Li~~~

The Universe of Brigit Markz

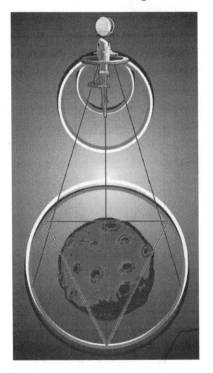

Book 2 in the Brigit Markz series

by Christopher E. Cancilla

This is

book number 2

in the

Brigit Markz Series

Life in Transition is a work of fiction and not based on any form of reality, including people, places, technology, situations, or things.

In this creative work, any resemblance to any person, from the past, present, or future, living or dead, is pure coincidence.

FEBRUARY 2024 – First Printing

Left blank by design

CHAPTER ONE

In the four-plus years since leaving the Hill Life community, Brigit and Joseph have been happy. They found a purpose to help humanity like they could never have imagined if they stayed at Hill Life. Their home is theirs, next to their now very close friends Gayle and Jon. David and Marissa brought a few items from the mountain house, as they refer to it, to help minimize her homesick feelings after leaving the settlement. The settlement believes that Brigit and Joseph died. They were memorialized by their friends. Neither of them has any family.

Brigit enjoys the short time milking her three cows, Bossy, Flossy, and Joan, every morning and evening. Joan is the wild one.

It may not be the hours from her previous life in the settlement but the time she calls her retreat. A retreat into the past, where she feels like she is a part of the community again.

Joseph is no different. His retreat is also with the animals. All animals. On their farm, he feeds and cares for a family of raccoons and opossums, cows, a pig, and a horse. Sometimes, he feels low, almost sad, and the horse or their cat snuggle with him until he feels better.

Brigit is an in-demand agricultural consultant throughout the solar system. Joseph is a sought-after animal and livestock consultant. They understand the dirt, the plants, and the animals like no one else. People find it hard to understand how they do what they do. The term plant or animal whisperer has been said but left on the roadside. They hope no one uses it again.

Marketing had a hand in their status as regional experts, and Magda and her team had a lot to do with it. Rufus Kap and his sister Maria were drafted into the fold as contractors, and they sometimes traveled and assisted Brigit with the plants and greenhouses in other worlds, which she refers to as the other settlements. Settlements of humanity. Rufus figured out that Brigit and Joseph had issues. He also asked one question, 'Where are you from, really?' He and his sister are now fully informed about the community. They have been sworn to secrecy.

The local veterinarian occasionally consults with Joseph when he gets a case that needs emotional fixing, like a depressed animal. Joseph teaches a class on identifying a depressed or sad animal, most likely a pet. He can ask the animal where it hurts, and Joseph gives the vet a place to start. They usually find the answer quickly after he arrives and spend time with the animal.

The oddest encounter he had was in New Zealand. A Rhino's mate was lost in the muck, and no one had any idea it was lost or where it was. The mate found Joseph and let him know. Others thought the Rhino was charging Joseph and nearly shot the animal. Joseph and the others followed the rhino. She led the group to the muck pit. It took quite a while, but they managed to pull him out with a winch and ropes and sprayed the mud off him. He put his head on Joseph's shoulder, and the mate did the same. The landowners, ranchers, and hands had never seen this before. They realized Joseph was very special to the animals and, therefore, to the owners. The owners of this land – this ranch –

have called on Joseph multiple times for assistance with the animals under his care.

Brigit and Joseph still work for Magda, now a four-star general in command of the solar systems team of services troubleshooters and safety inspectors. Her team has doubled in size, maybe a little more. Still, the core group, the original team members, are the only ones who know the true origin of Brigit Markz, Joseph Waters, and the others.

The chiefs and Mik still work for her, as does Lieutenant Reilley. As a Full General, she can field promote, with reason, as her Boss stated flatly to her one afternoon. The argument is that this usually is, by regulations, done under combat conditions. Since the solar system has not been at war in more than a century, General MagdaLynne Rochavarro exercised it, tested is the correct word, on him.

She ensured that his promotion was on Mars, in the dome where he grew up, and his sister was present to pin it on his uniform. It was a fantastic party and encompassed nearly all the dome's inhabitants.

The core group, the leadership team, the inner circle, the…. Brigit likes to have fun with Magda when she refers to their group. One time, she called them the Magda Club. She said it sounded better in her head.

Virginia and Rory were promoted to Warrant Officer 3 just under a year ago and should be there for a while.

Magda confidentially told Mik and Brigit, on a long flight from Mars to Mercury Station, to drop off supplies; she planned to promote them both to Captain since they had been doing the work of captains since day one and were doing it quite well. However, after speaking to her former boss, a retired general, about it, she realized it needed to be accomplished precisely and correctly, or it could be reversed. In the next few months, maybe she can get it done. As Mik stated, the Chiefs did not know why they were being ridden hard and put away wet. But, the women realized something was going on, and they took it all in stride and excelled.

Three years and six months after Magda promoted Mik to Major, Brigit was there when he received his orders to Lieutenant Colonel. She had a little fun with him, but in the end, nothing changed. She was still the Boss; he was number 2, and the chiefs were number 3, interchangeably. Depending on the moment, Joseph and Brigit fell within that group.

Magda had Mik and Rory each take out a ship and pick up everyone who worked for her for a meeting or conference in a new station in the asteroid belt. Since many smaller rocks have been mined or moved, there is ample space to put a station. The military station, called Asteroid Prime, is just that. A hollowed-out asteroid that has some gravity and enough room for a very large number of people.

Although considered a military base, it is more of an orbital platform, a jumping point out into the outer solar system by researchers and adventurers.

After these few years, the house, land, and farm Jon and Gayle Janning bought for Joseph and Brigit now has a lived-in and comfortable look and feel. They love this house and have personalized it as their home.

Brigit put names on the doors of her spare rooms, one for each team member. That hallway has six guest rooms similar, but a little larger, to Jon and Gayle's. Four rooms are permanently assigned to Magda, Mik & Monica Spencer, Rory Mitchell, and Virginia Rolf.

The last two rooms are available if needed, especially for visitors from the council of elders as they arrive for the collection or visitors who want a little escape into a different life.

Soon, it would be time for Ramona and Marshall to make the collection, and she would see her again. It has been nearly four years. Brigit also knows that Mark will be there, and a few weeks ago, she dreamt about a new romance in his life, Zoee Rathman. She is very happy for him.

The secret rooms under their kitchens were explored in depth by the Chiefs. They used interesting tools and found a tunnel between the two houses, perfect for bad weather or the winter months in Colorado. They learned tunnels were extended to the barns on each property and the neighbor's home on each side. It freaked out the neighbors when their kitchen counter opened, and some young people popped up. They all had a lot of fun playing with the new hidden path, but it was just another walkway. Perfect in inclement weather. The others, like Gayle and Brigit, use the underground area for storage and holding the canned or preserved items they create.

Brigit had a dream last night, a bad one. She saw the crops on the stations, Mars dying, and people hungry. They, the agro-departments on the five stations, researched the problem to death and could not resolve the issue. She dreamt about the problem, but not about the resolution. This is pretty odd since she would typically have the answer when she awakened.

She sat in her living room, concentrating on the dream, trying to force a resolution. She just kept reliving the same parts as she dreamt yesterday night. She laughed. Joseph hates it when she says yesterday night instead of last night.

RING!!

Brigit opened her eyes and looked at the screen, realizing she had sat there for nearly two hours.

"Answer."

The video lit up with Magda's face. "Hi, kid. Got a little job for you and Joseph. I need you to be on Mars – you leave in the morning – and Joseph on the far side lunar dome. I need you both up here at my station as early as possible."

"I know. We will be there at 0600." Brigit replied.

"You what…. Oh, never mind. Did you happen to see the fix?"

"No, just the problem. I guess I will need to get my hands dirty on this one," She paused, "Why is Joseph heading to the Moon?"

"There is a new vet on the moon that needs his consultation. Let's leave it at that for the moment."

"OK. We will be there in the morning and park our little car in your garage. Did I ever mention how much I like driving, flying, or whatever?"

"Several hundred times, actually. As for getting to your contract locations, Rory and Virginia are taking you to Mars in the new ship. Fresh off the production line, this is her shakedown. After dropping you off, they will do a scouting survey for a new station near Saturn or Neptune. You will have a few guests on the flight from Earth, but it should be pretty easy with an hour's flight time and barely enough time for you to nap. I'm looking forward to seeing how fast you can get there. They should return to you on Thursday and drop the rest of the group off on Mars, where their research will continue, and they can bring you home solo."

She took a drink from a coffee cup. Brigit noticed it was a regular cup, not a zero-G cup, and remembered her new office has gravity. Magda continued, "Joseph, on the other hand, has a fun trip. There is a rotation flight of fighters due to head to the moon in the morning at 1100 hours. He will sit backseat on one of them. Their boss owes me a favor, and I figured Joseph needed a little fun. He will do the same thing in a few days with the group heading home after their six-month rotation."

"He will like that!" Brigit smiled at the video.

"OK, gotta run. See you in the morning. By the way, can you bring a little milk for Fuzzy if the girls can spare it?"

"Of course I can." She waved to her friend and Boss, and the call disconnected. A moment later, "House, call Gayle."

"Hi, Brigit."

"Hi, Gayle. We need to head to the moon, for Joseph, and Mars, for me, very early tomorrow. Can you watch the house for a few days?"

"Of course. But they should be here in the collection by Friday. If I remember correctly, you said Ramona would be on this one, and I know you do not want to miss her."

"I don't, but this is important. I should be back a few hours before they arrive." She added, "Joseph, too."

"No problem. Just do what you need to do. Tell everyone we said HI and that they have not been here for a visit in quite a while. What about the queen of the house?"

"My little kitty? Serena will be just fine. She has a free run of the house, and food and water are there for her when needed. As for the box, she has a little door to go outside when needed. Besides, she'll be at your door if we're not home."

"True." She said, "I will keep my eye out. Besides, Magda and Marissa like talking to each other, so they will likely show up while they are here." She paused a heartbeat, "Gotta go pack. Thanks again."

The video disconnected, "House, call Joseph."

A few rings later, "Hi, Honey."

"I got a call from Magda…."

Joseph interrupted, "So did I. 0600. You fly with the kids. I fly in a fighter!"

"Oh, you already heard." She laughed at him.

"I did. I also heard on the way home that they cannot land at the station, so they would get close, and I needed to walk maybe half a mile or so." He grinned, "I really like zero-G operation, and it gives me the chance to improve. This time, I get a little air gun or something to blast my way to the open garage door."

"That does sound like fun!" She paused momentarily, "Tell me about it. It's the second thing when we get home." He knew what she meant.

He replied, "I added it to my calendar."

They talked for a few more minutes, and he told her he would be home in less than two hours. He was on the other side of the planet, in New

Zealand. Molesworth Station is the largest ranch on the planet, and they had a problem with all of their livestock. For the past few days, Joseph has been 'researching' the park, fields, barns, feed, water, and visitors to find the reason. Nothing!

Until he talked to a few of the children who said, "The sheeps were not friendly like last time she was here. They scared of somethin."

Joseph grabbed a little ground car and took off into the fields. It was beautiful here. He could definitely live here. Most of the day had passed, and the guy who had given him the car also gave him a small cooler. He said it had lunch he could take with him. A bushman's lunch. After driving around for a few hours, he stopped and sat under a tree.

Opening the cooler, he unwrapped the sandwich. Wheat bread, cheese, meat, and chips on the sandwich. Onion and cucumber were packed with a variety of flavors.

He took a bite, and his eyes opened. It was magnificent. He took some water and sat in the shade of the tree, enjoying his lunch. He really loves the springtime, and here it was spring. A short time later, he finished his lunch and was quite disappointed because he had finished the sandwich. He really wanted more. But, now that he saw it, he can make one at home.

He put all the trash into the cooler, hopped in the small open-topped car, and took off. About 45 minutes later, he found a few animals in the middle of the field. Shot with an antique black powder rifle. He knew about them; he had one above his fireplace in the community where he used to live. He dug the slug out of one sheep.

He reported it to the owners and returned to the field where most animals were huddled. He assured them the humans doing this would be stopped. Returning to the offices, he reported what he found. They went to collect the unfortunate members of this ranch. He gave them the coordinates of the unfortunate animals.

Joseph waited for them, and they removed the animals properly. He returned to the parking area and found the guy who gave him the cooler. Joseph discovered that the lunch he had was a traditional Kiwi classic that is eaten as a breakfast, a lunch, or a dinner. Anytime.

"Joseph," Liam said, "It's a whatever-you-have meal. Open the fridge, fill the sammy, and enjoy. Only one rule: anything goes!"

Joseph laughed, "I need to keep that in mind. Always have odd bits, as you call it, in the fridge."

They talked about food for a little longer, which was of interest to the two of them. It was time to quit for the day.

Joseph thanked him and scheduled his return flight home. Liam said the spaceport was on his way home and gave him a lift. It was maybe an hour's drive, and the time flew by. The conversation was excellent.

They thanked Joseph, and before heading to the terminal, he went to the animals in the visitor park to let them all know it was over. The little girl he spoke to was back, and he called over a small lamb her size. He said, "Give the lamb a hug." She did, and they were instant friends.

The park and petting zoo returned to regular operation before he boarded the transport home, and the former employee, wreaking havoc on the property, was sentenced to a year in the lunar prison with intense therapy and evaluation.

The next day, just before dawn, the authorities caught the person. A woman who used to work there but was terminated for not being friendly enough to work with the public was trying to deter people from visiting the park and the animals. She fessed up and said she was on the other side of the million-acre property, and there was no way they could have found her so easily.

She did not realize the animals had all passed her location on to Joseph. She appears one day and looks around. Returns the next morning before dawn and kills one of the animals. They told him where she was looking around that morning.

Brigit made dinner, Joseph's favorite meal. Something they first had with Magda. A cultural product no one in the community had ever had but would adore if they had the chance.

Joseph walked into the house and yelled, "Brigit, I'm home!"

She was in the closet behind the door he opened to enter the house. She did not say a word. All she did was knock on the door.

He closed the front door, and she stood there smiling. "How long have you been standing behind the door?" He asked.

"Only a moment since someone opened it and blocked me into the closet."

They hugged, and he sniffed, "Did you make…."

She grinned, "Yes, I did…."

He yelled, "Tacos!"

"Gayle and Jon will be here in 15 minutes. We are all having dinner together. Then we need to do a few chores, go to bed, and head to the station in the morning."

"Yes, dear. But I have a question. Go to bed sounds as though there is sleep in there somewhere."

She winked at him, "Now, get cleaned up and changed," She spanked his butt, "Our guests will be here in a few minutes."

He kissed her again and went to their room for a fast shower and clean clothes. Brigit set the table and finished making iced tea, and as she put the picture on the table, Gayle and Jon walked in.

"We're here, and I'm hungry!" Jon said.

"Me too! But she made me clean up before she would feed me," Joseph said as he walked into the living room and headed to the kitchen table.

"Children," Gayle said.

"Sit and eat. I made enough, Gayle. You can take the rest since we will not be here the rest of the week."

Jon said, "Hot Dog! Taco eggs in the morning!"

Joseph stopped, "That sounds good."

Brigit said, "We will eat at the station in the morning. We have to be there for a 6 a.m. departure. That's what 0600 means. We need to get up and leave well before 0530. Need me to translate that for you?"

"No. True, you leave at 6 a.m. I hang around till 10 a.m. Maybe I can grab Magda and get something after you and the kids take off."

Gayle said, "If you were to grab Magda, she would toss you across the room."

Everyone laughed as they grabbed shells and made their dinner.

Jon asked, "How was New Zealand?"

"Pretty sad, actually. As we were landing in Denver, I got a message that a woman had been fired and was taking her revenge on the animals in hopes that the tourists would stop patronizing the park. I figured it out, and it is all fixed." He paused momentarily, "I found a new food, Bushman's Sammy. A sandwich. Whatever you got between bread. Spaghetti, meat, cheese, anything goes."

Jon stopped and looked at him, "Spaghetti sandwich. I'll keep that in the back of my mind for later use."

The conversation changed to the arrival of the visitors at the end of the week, which could be as early as Thursday but most likely on Friday.

The council knows how to use the little comm unit and where the particular box is located. In the past years, they, as in Gayle and Brigit, upgraded the cabin to include gear similar to the cave. The comfort level has drastically improved for those on the path.

When they arrive at the cabin, Marissa will call and tell them they arrived safely.

The remainder of the evening was dinner, iced tea, and fellowship. However, they watched a new comedy on the video together and have never laughed like that in recent history.

CHAPTER
TWO

"Hill Farm, this is the cabin." A female voice said over the comm system.

Gayle replied, "Cabin, this is Gayle. How are you doing?"

"A bit cold, hungry, but otherwise, we are all fine."

"I'll make a guess. Ramona, Marshall, Mark, and you?" Gayle said, smiling.

"Yep, tell Brigit she was correct. As usual. We will spend the night and be there around dinner tomorrow." Marissa said.

"I will let her know. She is … Uh…. out of town at the moment, but she is due back around lunchtime tomorrow. So, perfect timing."

"Brigit and I were up there last week. We added a few things to the pantry. Enjoy. Also, the Chiefs changed out the cots and sleeping bags since it was getting colder. You all should be very warm and comfortable tonight. Jon put a lock on the door inside. Have a good rest, and see you tomorrow for dinner. I'm making a chicken pot pie."

"My favorite. The others are looking at me funny. I'll explain it to them later. By the way, did you happen to put any tea in the pantry?"

"Yes, dear. I thought of you. Earl Gray decaffeinated. A whole box of it. A small flask of spirits also goes well with the tea."

"I may just give it a try. It sounds perfect for an after-dinner dessert." She paused a moment, "OK, I need to eat. We will call you again when we leave in the morning. Cabin out."

"Understood. Talk to you in the morning."

"Home. Call Brigit, Jon, Joseph, and Magda on a conference call."

A few moments later, all of their faces appeared on the screen.

"They just arrived at the cabin. I expect them to be here by dinner tomorrow. CPP for dinner. Magda, you bring the wine."

"You got it!"

"Brigit and Joseph, you make it here by then?"

Brigit said, "I'll tell the kids to not spare the horses."

Joseph added, "Not a problem. I should be dirtside around 1 p.m."

"Perfect. Talk to you all then." They all disconnected except for Jon. "Just you and me."

"Need anything from town?"

"Yes, actually. All the fixins for chicken pot pie."

Jonathan laughed and said, "Understood. Stopping at the grocery store. Send me a list."

"Yes, honey. You know I love you?"

"Yes, I do. As long as I run your errands for you." He laughed a little, as did Gayle, "See you in a bit." He disconnected and turned his truck around to head back into town to pick up dinner.

~~~~~~~~~~~

"Hill Farm, this is Cabin."

"Go ahead, darlin'," Jon said.

"I hope Gayle doesn't get the wrong impression?" The others, Mark, Marshall, and Ramona, just looked at her.

"I am here too," Gayle said.

They heard laughter through the comm. "OK, perfect. The time is 9 a.m., and we are leaving. See you between 4 and 5."

"Understood. Thanks for the warning," Jon said, "You know where to park."

Jon asked, "How are the new beds?"

"Warm, comfortable, and did I mention warm?" Marissa said. You could see the smiles through the call.

"Excellent. See you when you get here," Gayle said.

"Cabin out."

Last night, Marissa explained the comm, the food, and the beds to everyone. They were amazed at their comfort; the dinner was simple to prepare and tasty.

"Home, call Joseph and Brigit."

"Hi, Gayle." They both said.

Joseph said, "I am leaving the moon at noon. Flight time is about an hour, so I should arrive at the station at 1300."

Brigit added, "We are prepping for launch and should hit space shortly. Scheduled ETA is 1315, according to the Wonder Chiefs."

"Wonder Chiefs. Can't wait to hear about that one. OK, I'll wait at the station, and we can fly home together." Joseph said.

"Good. Because falling from orbit is fine, but that sudden stop at the end may get a little uncomfortable."

"Uh Huh," Gayle said, "Let me know when you land." She disconnected.

~~~~~~~~~~~

"Brigit. We have a little issue we need to correct. You can go grab a snack if you want?" Virginia said through the comm system.

They were on the ship doing the preflight, and Brigit was in the bay walking to the ship.

"There's a little snack bar just outside the bay. I'll head there and get a coffee and a Danish. You two want anything?" She asked.

"Actually, yes. What you said sounds great!" Rory replied.

"Me too!" Virginia added.

"OK, see you in a few. Cheese, cherry, or apple danish? I'll be in my suit, so call me if you need me or when you correct the issues."

"Understood," They said together. Then both added, "Cheese danish."

Brigit turned right and headed down a hall. Walking out through the side entrance. She is very familiar with the Mars landing bay and most people who work in and near the bay.

She walked into the snack bar and waited in line. One of the employees called next.

"Yes, Ma'am, what can I get you?" He asked

"Let's see. Three large vanilla lattes, medium sweet, with a shot. Three cheese Danish," she said. She looked in the case and saw the largest chocolate chip cookie, "…and that cookie!"

The guy turned and made the drinks and put them in a little carrier. He put the Danish and the cookie into a sealed sleeve. Adding the zero-G cover to the coffee cups, Brigit smiled.

She put her ID on the register, and it chirped the payment was accepted. She added a tip and picked it all up.

She headed back to the bay and walked slower than usual. Arriving at the side door where she left, she stood momentarily in front of the airlock.

As she did, someone stood behind her and spoke, "Sorry, Ma'am. That is a sealed door. You must enter the bay through the office complex or the passenger reception desk. You need special clearance to use this door." She recognized the voice.

She put her ID on the panel, and the airlock cycled. She pulled on the door, and it opened. Then, she turned, and for the first time, the voice knew it was her.

"Brigit! Why did you let me rant on like that?"

"Well, Colonel. I just was not thinking straight. I need my coffee!"

"Obviously. All three of them?"

"No. One is mine. The others are for the Chiefs."

He smiled, "Where are they?"

"On the ship doing a preflight. There was a glitch, and I went for snacks."

"Perfect. Don't let on, but I'll be there in a few minutes to say hello. I have not seen them in almost a year."

"Understood Colonel." She said.

"What did I tell you about the Colonel thing?"

"Sorry, Magnus." She stood in the airlock, and he closed the airlock door. As it sealed, the inner door opened when the pressure equalized. In the airlock, she also picked up her helmet from the shelf. It's a better option than carrying it around the base.

She strolled to the ship and walked in. Sitting in the back seating area was someone she did not know.

"Hello?"

"Hello, Brigit."

"OK, you know me, but I do not know you." She looked at him again, "You're not wearing a pressure suit?"

"Correct. Don't need one. Are you sure you don't know me?"

"Oh my god, Brad!" It hit her. It had not happened in a while, about four years ago, watching the sunrise on the last day on Mars.

"That's me."

"Why are you visiting me?"

"I am about to move on. Serena already did. I suppose you understand she set all of this in motion by pushing you to Magda, who caught you on the first flight."

"I do understand that, yes."

"Before I move on, I want you to know that I still love you after all we have been through. I have always loved you. But, as you can plainly see, I realized that too late. I also wanted you to know that I like Joseph. He is the perfect person for you to spend the rest of your very long life together."

She grinned at her dead first husband, "How long of a life?"

"Well, we do have rules. Let's just say long. I also want you to know that a group is mapping the entire planet. They are about to cover the settlement, and once they do, they will visit and ruin it all. You and the others need to meet them on the path near Joseph's cave. Bring Magda and those two," He thumbed at the cockpit.

Brigit looked toward where he was motioning out of instinct and saw them both staring at her.

"Don't worry, you two, I'm not crazy. But, I am talking to my dead husband."

"OK?" Virginia said.

"No, really."

Brad said, "Tell them to grab a book, open it, and point to some text. I will see what they are pointing to and tell you, and you can repeat it to them."

"Rory, grab one of the books next to you, open it to a random page, and point to a paragraph. Brad will read it to me, and I will recite it."

Rory grabbed a book, opened it, and pointed to a three-sentence paragraph.

"Three sentences," Brad said.

"Good, only three sentences," she said after Brad told her what to say.

"OK. We believe you and that there is a ghost on the ship." Virginia said.

"He is not fond of the term ghost. But it is accurate."

Brad said, "Thanks."

Brigit looked at the chiefs, "Give us just a minute."

They walked into the cockpit, and a few minutes later, Brigit called to them.

"Brigit, you are freaky, but in a good way," Rory said.

"Once we are in space, I need a secure connection to Magda."

"Is it what the ghost, I mean Brad, said?"

"It is."

The Colonel boarded the ship, "Hi, gang!"

"Hi, Colonel. Need a lift?" Rory asked.

"No. Just thought I would say hello. Ain't seen you two in a while. Saw her in the airlock." He paused, "How did the survey mission go?"

Rory said, "Smooth. I think they found a couple likely places to park a station. If I heard right, the Moons we looked at are not hospitable. But, a mining team can head there to get the fuel and minerals needed for those stations."

"I heard," He said, "They call the two of you the Wonder Chiefs. According to the survey team, the two of you set up, fixed, and calibrated the equipment and found exactly what they were looking for. One of the scientists said you two are all that and a bag of chips!"

"Not all that impressive, sir. Just stuff we know how to do to make the job easier." Virginia said.

Rory grinned and spoke, "Do we get a bonus!"

"Chief, if it was in my power, yes. But, sadly, work in the military is behind the proverbial curtain, so no one usually sees what we do. My heartfelt congratulations to both of you and I hope Miss Plant Whisperer here can figure out what is happening with the plants."

"I will make it my top priority, Magnus," Brigit said.

"Excellent. I'll let you fly off. I needed a non-science-team take on it."

"Well, Sir. If you need the flight attendant's opinion, that group will be happy at both locations. I overheard that there is enough stuff on the moons to last the stations for centuries. The trick will be mining the moons in the radiation and low gravity. They said it may need to be a new tech developed first. I told them they needed a tank to land, dig, and return to the station. I think they liked it."

"Interesting idea…." He walked off and yelled back from the bottom of the ramp, "Have a nice flight." A moment later, the thunderous voice of the Colonel, "BIFF! Let's get these people on their way."

The airlock doors on the ship closed, and the ramp slid away.

"Yes, sir." Biff's voice was heard. "Getting my former boss the hell out of here." Virginia laughed, and a moment later, their clearance and launch instructions, the familiar beeps, and the dome opening. They were on their way home.

Preflight was faster than normal since they were almost done when they found the glitch. After replacing the connector, everything was good.

They launched, left Mars space as usual, and kicked it into high gear.

Fifteen minutes out of Mars, Virginia called Magda, "What's up, Chief?"

"General, please secure your side of the connection."

A moment later, "OK. Talk!"

Brigit took over and reiterated the conversation with Brad.

"A department is high-res mapping the entire planet. They are in Colorado now, about to scan the mountains. If they see the settlement, life there will change."

"How do you know this?"

Virginia said, "Trust me, Boss, it is accurate. We can tell you that later, but you must know this is 100% accurate for now."

"OK. I will look into it."

"Actually. We have a plan. In a month, all of us will meet the group at the cave. That is their base camp area. Marissa and Mark will inform the council, but I think I must go to the settlement eventually. Maybe I can live in both worlds, and the collections can simply be a shopping trip."

"OK. Talk to you about this at dinner." She disconnected.

"Are we at top speed?" Brigit asked.

A minute later, "We are now!" Rory said.

Virginia said, "ETA to the station is 33 minutes."

CHAPTER THREE

Joseph made it to the moon after taking care of his assignment. He really likes the moon, and the people are friendly, like on Mars.

"Mr. Waters, you all strapped in?"

"I am, Commander, and my name is Joseph."

"Gocha. The name here is also Joseph. " He paused momentarily and flipped a few switches, "Have you ever been in a fighter?"

"Once, getting here a few days ago. It was faster than a shuttle, but it felt like my car. Looking forward to it, though."

"OK. A few rules. Never touch the controls, so keep your hands in your lap and your feet as far back as possible. Please turn off the mic if you need to use the little bag. Don't press any buttons. Leave your suit on the entire trip. Connect the suit to ship air; the red tube goes to the red connector, and the blue tube goes to the blue connector. In the event of an emergency, I will hit the eject. If you hear me say eject, eject, eject, squeeze your arms, knees, and feet together and hands under your armpits."

"Interesting and understood," Joseph said to his pilot.

"Lunar Flight Control to VP squadron leader. You are cleared to exit the bay. Assembly point is on you, 55 miles off the surface."

"Control, this is VP Leader, WillCo. 13 fighters are departing the station bay with 14 souls."

"VP Leader, 13 craft with 14 souls confirmed. Clear to launch."

"VP Leader to fighters, launch by the numbers." He paused and flipped a couple switches.

The flight leader, the ship's pilot where Joseph was sitting, said, "One Away!" He jetted out of the bay to the assembly point.

The others launched, and as they left the bay, they called out their flight number.

A minute or two later, all were in space and in a circle above, below, and around the leader.

"Control, VP Leader. Assembly complete."

"Leader, Control. Clear to head to your destination. Maintain 50,000 miles per hour for 4 minutes; cruising speed is at your discretion." There was a slight pause, "Godspeed, good flight."

"Leader to flight. Let's give my passenger something to talk about when he gets home. Max burst for 15 seconds, trim to 50k for 4 minutes, then go to 75% power." He paused.

"Leader from navigator, that will put us in Earth orbit in 13 minutes. I'm pretty sure he will enjoy the ride." A slight pause, "Navigation to Flight, power to max in three…. Two…. One…. NOW!"

Joseph thought to himself, THIRTEEN MINUTES! Holy Mackerel!

The grin on his face said it all.

~~~~~~~~~~~

"Joseph, I must tell you that your Boss said to give you a new experience. So, in five minutes, we will be a mile from the station where she lives. We were told you would exit the craft and fly naked – as in no ship – to the garage. To help you get there, you get the flashlight."

"Yep, she mentioned it to me. Are you talking about this thing in front of me on the console?"

"Yep, that's it. Now, here's how it works. There is a big end and a small end. The big end points to where you were, and the little one is where you want to go. There are two buttons on the case. The front button, the red one, is a laser, and the back button, the black one, turns on the jet. Press the front button and point it at the garage or train the bright red dot on the space above the garage door. Press the jet-on button while keeping the laser trained at the point of entry. The jet will only run for three seconds at a press. One press will get you to a fast walking speed. I like three presses; as you get close, you can turn it around and tap it lightly to slow down. You can step softly into the garage standing if you get good at it. If you notice, it fits into the side of your hip, so where you are facing, the laser will hit."

"Got it. It sounds easy enough. I enjoy zero-G operation and practice in the center chamber every chance." Joseph said to his pilot.

"OK, opening canopy. Have fun!" The canopy opened, and Joseph unstrapped.

"This is rather unnerving," He said more to himself than anyone else. Floating out of the ship, he realized he was not moving, but the ship was dropping slowly away. He pressed the laser button, trained it on the plating above the door, and pressed the jet button. "Note to self. It really looks different than when you are arriving in the car." It took him a moment to get it recentered, but he pressed it a second time, and although he did not feel like he was moving, he knew he was flying at a pretty fast pace.

It took him several minutes to get near the opening, but he was on track to hit the garage door dead center. The garage door rolled up as he approached, and he hit the opening as he thought. Turning the device around, he tapped the jet button and came to a dead stop twenty feet above the bay floor. He pointed the laser end down, tapped the button, and landed on the floor where the mag boots connected.

"Joseph, are you sure you have never done this before? That was perfect!"

"Thanks, Joseph. Did not know I had an audience."

As he said that, the rest of the flight all cheered for him. In the garage, the door closing slowly, he waved to the ships watching him, and as he bowed, the door closed and sealed.

"Well, my friend, I not only like to bring my date home, but I like to ensure they are safe inside the house. I hope to fly with you again; you are interesting to talk to. Flight, best speed home, Nav, lead the way." The ships all departed.

Several techs came out clapping their hands. A man, obviously in charge, said, "Mr. Waters, that was impressive for your first time." They finished applauding for him, and the guy said, "The General is expecting you. You hungry?"

"I am, yes," Joseph said.

"Let's get you out of that suit. I have your spare clothing here."

~~~~~~~~~~~

Joseph walked into the conference room, where he had been multiple times. Sitting there was a hot, perfectly prepared steak, mashed potatoes, and brussel sprouts covered in garlic butter. On the other side of the table were Mik, a steak in front of him, and Magda, a steak in front of her.

To his right were two more steaks, and to his left was a single plate.

"OK, perfect. I take it the kids and Brigit are arriving?" He said.

Before anyone could answer, the three walked into the room and sat in their places.

"EAT! Then we will chat. You need to head home since you will have visitors shortly." Magda said, "Oh, Brigit, here is a vid of Joseph walking home from his trip to the Moon." She replayed the last couple minutes of the vid, and he did not realize he was talking to himself so much.

Brigit stood there watching intently as her husband approached, entered the garage, soft landed on the floor, and bowed to the flight leader, who was now roughly 30 feet outside the hangar door. She applauded and sat next to Joseph, and they kissed hello.

"Brigit, I looked into what you said, you are correct. There is a team remapping the Earth."

Joseph asked, "…and…"

Brigit answered, "…and they will discover the settlement, get curious, and visit. Disrupting the entire community."

"Did you have a dream?" He asked.

Virginia replied, "Well, not exactly."

Joseph gave her a very curious look, "Huh?"

Brigit was silent for a moment, then looked at Joseph, "Brad told me. The mapping team is on a station referred to as Station 11. A tiny station in Earth orbit."

Joseph's face took on a serious look, "Magda, what can we do about it?"

"I simply love how you hear Brigit got classified news from a man who has been dead more than four years, and you simply take it in stride and move on," Magda said. Mik had not heard of this before, so he stopped mid-chew and listened intently. Magda continued, "He's not in the room, right?" Brigit shook her head. Magda continued, "I made a few discreet inquiries and found the department doing the remapping. They started at the Mississippi River and went east around the globe. They mapped the planet and verified the results with a team of six people for over a year. Each has 30 degrees of latitude, and each section they scan takes about a month." She paused and looked at each person.

She continued, "After inquiring about a specific section of the planet, I received a message to report to a point in space between the Earth and Mars. Took about ten minutes to get there, and I was told to come alone in a small craft. I used your car," she said to Brigit, who smiled. "I parked in their bay. Can you imagine my shock and surprise when I met with ambassadors, delegates, generals, and people? I had no idea who they were, nor did they tell me. But boy, howdy, they knew everything about me!" She paused.

Continuing, "The conversation, no, not conversation. It was a stern warning and a welcome to a tiny club. They told me only a dozen, including me, knew the community existed. In the past, they have protected its anonymity from whatever they could." She grinned, "They were unaware of the mapping detail, which shocked me. I fessed up and took a page from Brigit. The truth is the best policy, so they know about all of us: you, Joseph, Gayle, and Jon. I told them about Mik and Monica, and yes, you two also," she pointed to the chiefs.

Magda sipped her drink, "To be honest, I thought I would be executed or something, but once I told them about the vision thing and a few other things you can all do, the tone of the meeting changed to more of a conference," She took another sip, "I wish this was scotch right now," She said under her breath, continuing, "Denver is about the 40-degree mark, and the person scanning that area is someone named," She looked at a portapad, "Marcel Romet, Lieutenant Commander." She smiled, "Figures, Navy."

"Marcel Romet?" Rory said. Pronouncing it differently, but most likely correctly.

They all just looked at her, so she finished the thought.

"Marcel and I had a thing. Maybe a few years ago. We both took a vacation in the Bahamas, had rooms next to each other, and hit it off near the pool. It was a two-week stay, and we never discussed what we did. We just talked about the day, the future, where we grew up, and things like that. On the last day, it was time to head home, and we were both dressed in our uniforms. I was a freshly minted Warrant Officer 2, and he was a Navy Lieutenant soon to be a Lieutenant Commander." She paused and smiled.

Virginia poked her in the arm.

"Sorry, we got really close but have not had the time to visit each other in the past six months."

Brigit had an idea, "Rory, can you send an invite to Marcel to invite him to the farm next week? As little information as possible, please. Maybe we can get him to clean that section and make it look like what is there is not."

"I get it," Mik said.

Virginia said, "I can grab the scans and replace them with the cleaned version.

"No!" Magda said, "If this happens, Marcel must do it. Tag lines, signatures, approvals. There is a lot of red tape when a planet is scanned and mapped. If the I's are not dotted and the T's crossed properly, it shoots up red flares that higher-ups see. Besides, my new friends mentioned no one in the chain from Marcel up is aware of the community."

Rory said, "I will send him a message. I know he's off duty on Friday and Saturday. He can spend the night, and we can tell him why we need it all classified. The big question. How much information do we pass on to him?"

"Be honest. Best policy." Brigit said.

Magda said, "If that doesn't work, I will get the brass to set a classified level on that section."

Brigit asked, "Magda, can you answer a question I have wondered about for quite a while? You mention the Navy and the rest of the military as if there were more."

Magda smiled, "About a hundred years ago, the branches all consolidated, merged. Since the Navy makes it sound like they are on the water, protecting us, they are in space protecting us. The other branches, like Army, Marines, Air Force, and Space Force, merged into the Consolidated Services. Before the merge, those branches used the same ranking system, like Lieutenant, Major, and General; most had a Warrant Officer program designed as a path for enlisted personnel to become commissioned. The Navy, on the other hand, had its ranks and stayed as they were. So, the rank of Lieutenant Commander is equal to that of a Major. A commander is a Lieutenant Colonel and an Admiral is equivalent to a General."

Mik continued, "The only sorta similar one is Captain. But, as you know, a captain is the third officer rank. In the Navy, it is the sixth. Therefore, a Navy Captain is equal to a Colonel. He paused, "Leadership of the services went from six people ultimately running the military to three. Navy Commandant, CS Commandant, and Services Commandant. They lead and decide by a committee of three. Every huge decision needs to be unanimous, and they do pretty well. There are multiple sub-departments, areas of expertise, and covert operations. However, the Navy must maintain a warrior aspect and train the other branches to fight. They have the ships, we have the people. So, in reality, nothing really changed. If you are interested, we are under the Services Commandant."

"Last question," Joseph asked, looking at Magda, "Where are you on the pyramid?"

Magda thought momentarily, and Mik said, "Well, the Boss here is like the number four person in the Sol system. She has few above her and just about everyone below her."

"I have six above me, Mik. That's why my days are filling with meetings, and my inspection times are getting less and less. I love the inspection times, but the kids here and Mik are the leaders in the inspection teams. The teams they manage are located on Mars, the Moon, and the station. They all still need to do an on-site inspection at least twice a year somewhere, and I am also thinking of making that mandatory for me. When can we all head out for an inspection?"

Virginia said, "Boss, I have an on-site on Mars in a few months. It was not the base but the new station they had just finished. How about the initial inspection of a brand new station?"

Magda grinned, "Set it up. Add it to my calendar. Set up the quarters, the flight, everything."

"By then, Brigit will be licensed as a pilot, so I can set this up for her check ride. Mik and Rory can evaluate my recommendations, and you can issue the license."

They talked a bit more about the flight, being a pilot, and Joseph leaving the hard flying to his wife. He said it gives him the time to take a nap and that she loves flying and has everything to do with it.

Joseph grinned, "But Magda, my friend, my pal, my Boss. If you ever want someone on the team trained in the operation of one of those fighters, I volunteer."

"If that ever happens, Joseph, it's all yours," Magda said, "You two need to head downstairs.

You have visitors arriving soon." During the conversation, they finished their food.

Virginia added, "Looks like maybe ninety minutes at their current speed." She brought up a vid of the cart heading to the farm.

"OK, I have a couple things I need to do, then fly home," Brigit said, "Can you print out a picture of the cart?"

A second later, "Done. I'll bring it to the dinner."

"Me too. I have a few errands to run myself. Meet you in the bay in an hour?" Joseph said to his wife.

"Perfect!" She replied. "So, Virginia, how is our little car doing? That thing is an antique, a collector's item."

"I know," Joseph said. "Last time I flew it, I had several offers to buy it. But I like that little car, and our mechanic is amazing."

"I like working on it, and by the way, I upgraded the engine last time it was here. It's got a little more speed and is smoother now. Take your friends to the moon in half an hour or Mars in 5. There is enough room for four comfortably, five if you are friendly." Virginia paused, "And the best part is that no pressure suit is required. Dome to dome flights."

"Wonderful. I just may do that," Brigit said.

Joseph stood, as did Brigit, "OK, gotta run."

Magda said, "Dinner is at Gayle's farm, and dessert is on me. Her dining table is bigger."

CHAPTER FOUR

Brigit and Joseph entered the atmosphere slowly, not much of a fireball this time. She is getting better at reentry.

"Denver Landing control, this is car 324 breaching the atmosphere."

"Hi, Brigit. Heading home?"

"Yes, Kurt. ETA about 4 minutes."

"OK, you have straight in clearance. Nothing in your way."

"Thanks," She paused a heartbeat, "How's Carol and the family, Kurt?"

"Doing great. The kids always ask when they can go to the farm again?"

"Two weeks. We'll be out for a few days and have visitors for a week. You can all spend the night in two weeks and help with the 5 am chores. The kids are big enough now. What are they, eleven and nine?"

"Yep. They sure are. OK, I'll let them know when I get home tonight, and I'll need to ask for some time off. Joey likes feeding the animals, and Zoe thinks milking the cows is fun."

"Understood. Tell them I have a few new critters for them to play with. Besides, Serena will give them the grand tour when they get here," She paused, "See you in a couple weeks, Brigit in car 324 out."

She landed on the apron outside the barn and drove inside. The doors were already open; Jon had opened them a little bit ago.

Parking, she powered the car down to let it cool off. They got out, grabbed their bags, and headed towards the house.

"Man, it's good to be home!" They both said.

They were in two different places consulting. They recruited Rufus' sister as a part-time greenhouse consultant. Because of them, food was becoming abundant throughout the solar system.

They sat in their living room, both ready for a nap this afternoon, and the comm rang. Brigit answered, "Hello?"

"They're here!" And the line went dead.

Without speaking, they both jumped up and sprinted next door. "WOW!" Brigit said, "That was the best 5-minute rest I had in a while." Joseph started laughing as they ran out of the house.

They made it to the porch as the cart hit the apron.

The four sat on the cart, a familiar sight to two families. Before the cart came to a stop, Ramona yelled.

"Aunt Brigit!"

"Ramona, have I got things to show you."

Ramona replied, "I know." They hugged and went into the house. Ramona was staying in her mother's and Brigit's old room. Her husband Marshall was with her. They replaced the bed with a larger bed. They knew what was happening would happen.

Brigit planned to bring them to the station for lunch with Magda, then dinner, possibly on the moon. The next day, they arranged for a pilot and flight attendant to fly them to the moon for a day and a half before they headed home. She had already arranged to get everything they needed for this collection, and when they returned, they had no idea how they knew. Ramona simply said, "Aunt Brigit has the gift of dreams. She just knows."

No one questioned it. They found a few more things and will head home a few days later. Twice a year, she met with her friends from the community.

"How is everyone back home? How's your baby?" Brigit asked Ramona.

"BABY! She'll be five next month." She told her Aunt Brigit a little quieter as they walked into the house, "She has our gift also. Stronger than mine, maybe you too."

"Really? That is amazing."

"Speaking of which, my daughter, Serena Brigit, told me to tell you hello. She also gave this drawing to me to give to you." Ramona paused briefly to emphasize her daughter's ability, "Powerful, strong gift. She also wanted me to tell you the corn has worms, whatever that means, and because you know that, the food will be good."

"I never considered worms as the issue. I will call later and ask them to check."

"Where is this corn?" Marshall asked.

"On Mars. It makes sense that a worm was caught up in the dirt we brought from Iowa and is thriving on Mars. It will be easy to rid the field of worms." She got an evil grin, "All we need to do is introduce a few birds." She laughed.

Ramona handed Brigit the drawing. Brigit opened the folded paper and looked at it. She started crying.

It was her floating in the shuttle on her very first flight to the station all those years ago. You could see Joseph standing there with a smile on his face and Magda with her arms out, about to catch her. Behind her, she saw what looked like an angel. A figure standing or hovering with angel wings watching over her. Looking closer, she noticed the angel was Serena. The angel was pushing the floating out-of-control Brigit toward Magda. If you took great stock in the dreams as the community members, then it can only mean that Serena put this entire life into motion for her and Joseph.

Brigit broke down. Her sister was always with her. On the bench on Mars, her sister Serena told her that she had set this life for her in motion. She was bored in the community, but she settled.

Serena wanted her to experience what she needed to experience. The universe needed her, and Serena made sure the universe had Brigit.

A car landed in front of the cart. It was the five. Magda was driving, and Rory, Virginia, Mik, and Monica exited the vehicle.

Marissa was still on the porch, and Magda yelled at her. They hugged as if they were old friends.

Magda spoke from the steps. "Three new council members. Is that a record?"

"Yes, it is," Marissa said.

Mark asked, "They know who we are?"

Magda replied, "Yes, we do. We keep tabs on your settlement, and if something terrible ever happens, we will drop in and help so your people will think we are from a neighboring town."

Marissa added, "The other council members know this and have specific things to set in motion if we need their help. They will not drop in but close and walk in to help us. Two years ago, in that bad snow, the group who brought the kiln-dried wood so the settlement didn't freeze was them," She pointed to Mik and Rory.

"If I remember correctly, you wanted to trade excess wood for meat," Mark said, "I thought you two looked familiar."

"That's right," Magda said, "They took some meat, and we had a nice dinner here at the farm, thank you."

Marshall said, "Isn't that dangerous for us? People knowing about our community?" It got really quiet; everyone was listening.

"Not at all. Let's head into the house and grab some coffee. I'll explain," Gayle said.

They all sat around the table, and everyone introduced themselves. The coffee was ready, and everyone had a cup for the conversation.

"You were saying?" Mark said to Magda.

Brigit handed Magda the picture drawn by Ramona's daughter.

"Oh, dear lord!" She understood, "I take it the artist has your gift also."

Ramona replied, "My daughter. Yes, she does. You know about that, too?"

"Well, yes. There are a few other things as well. For example, I know that Brad appeared to Brigit on the way home from Mars yesterday, or was it this morning? Brad told her that a secret group was mapping the planet in a new, high-resolution scan. This is bad for the community. Once they see the structures, they will send a team to investigate. She informed me, and I found the person we needed to talk to. As a matter of fact, Rory here has a date with him next week and is spending the night next door. We hope to have him remove the community and make it appear like there is nothing there but trees."

They sat there in shock, staring at Magda.

"So, who's hungry?" Gayle asked.

No one moved.

~~~~~~~~~~~

Morning chores were completed, and they were all eating breakfast. The five-person team was still there, and they enjoyed helping out on the farm.

"You all work the farm as well. I thought you were all some kind of super technical team or something," Ramona said.

Magda added, "Well, I love working with the horses. Rory enjoys the chickens. Virginia likes milking the cows."

"I like working with my hands," Virginia said.

Magda continued, "Mik and Monica are the kitchen crew." She paused, "Let's see. You four are in three rooms in this house. The rest of us are next door at Brigit and Joseph's."

"You make it sound like an everyday occurrence?" Marshall said.

"In a way, it is. The Jannings and the Markz-Waters are dear and close friends to all of us. There is nothing we wouldn't do for them. Brigit has saved the crops on multiple stations around the solar system, the moon, and Mars. Believe it or not, people like her. Joseph talks to animals, and because of his ability to see things in the animals, he is a silent and sought-after consultant to all things furry. Including my baby!" She looked at Joseph, "I think Fuzzy wants you to visit soon. You'll probably get an earful about me, so be kind."

Joseph laughed. "I'll pop in tomorrow afternoon. Can one of the kids give me a ride?"

"Sure thing. Besides, the station vet needs to talk to you while you're there. Consulting hours!"

"Aunt Brigit, why did you never change your last name to Waters? It is the way we normally do it once we commit."

"I suggested to her that she not," Magda said, "In this world, my world, she is well known as Brigit Markz, and Joseph is known as Joseph Waters. It is also a well-known fact that they are a couple. There is no reason for her to change her last name. So, when the two of them show up for a job, the people are happy because they feel like they are getting two for the price of one. These two are happier, as is the person getting the aide."

Joseph said, "A real 2fer."

Virginia laughed, "Boss, I can safely say that everyone on your team is a trip."

"True," Magda said.

It got quiet for a minute. "Who's up for a day trip to the Moon?" Brigit asked.

Ramona raised her hand fast, and Marshall tentatively raised his. "Got one more seat?" She said.

They all looked at Marissa, who said, "Not me; I want to relax." She looked at Mark, "You want to go to the Moon and play for a few hours?"

"Is it safe?" He asked.

"Silly question. Yes, it's safe, and I am a good driver," Brigit answered.

Magda said, "She really is a good driver, I mean pilot."

"In that case, sure. I'm game," Mark replied.

The rest of the afternoon, the group talked. They love it when the council members come because they catch up on the important things they miss at home.

The five went back to the station. They had things to do in the morning. Current and prior settlement members talked away for a better part of the morning. Brigit took Mark and Marshall to meet Rufus.

Marissa and Gayle brought Ramona to the fabric store.

Everyone had a lot of fun and picked up things they needed.

They returned to the farms at about 10 pm, had a nice cup of tea, sat by the fire, and continued talking. Around midnight, they went to their homes or their rooms.

~~~~~~~~~~~

Gayle and Brigit were in the kitchen of Gayle's house, standing at the counter sipping coffee. Ramona walked into the room.

"You're up early?" Gayle said.

"The last two weeks, I was on milking. So, my body got used to early mornings." She pointed to a cup. They got the message. She sipped the coffee, "This is really good. It tastes different than what we have at home."

"This is commercially produced coffee, preground, roasted, and ready to use in the coffee maker," Gayle said. She walked to the fridge and picked out a bottle, "It comes in a concentrated liquid form also."

She made Ramona an iced latte of sorts. Heavy cream and milk, coffee concentrate, and liquid sugar. She put a few drops of vanilla and stirred it with some ice. She poured it into a glass, leaving all the ice behind, and added a straw.

Ramona accepted the glass and took a tentative sip. Her eyes opened wide. She liked it.

"Kiddo," Brigit said, "This is like drinking two or three cups of coffee when you are talking about the caffeine content. But I like these in the afternoon."

Gayle asked, "Last two weeks?"

"Yes. The person I was supposed to replace broke her hand. I volunteered for two weeks to help out. I really love getting up early and being with the girls, as Aunt Brigit used to call them."

"You remember that?" Brigit said.

"I do. I think you and Mom instilled in me the respect for animals."

She finished the cold drink and sipped from her warm cup. "Can I help you out with the morning chores?"

"Yes, you can." Brigit grinned, "Do you want to milk the cows?"

They all started laughing.

~~~~~~~~~~~

Brigit pulled the car from the barn and parked it on the apron in front of her porch. She returned to the house and grabbed an overnight bag in case they spent the night on the moon.

Ramona and Marshall walked through the bushes and to the car.

"Put your bags in the back, the trunk," Brigit said from inside the house. The weather was cooling off, and the windows were open. The cool air felt good.

"Sure thing," Marshall said as he took his wife's bag and stared at the trunk, trying to figure out how to open it. He saw the handle, grabbed it, and it popped. He placed his and his wife's bag in the trunk, and Mark walked up, tossed his bag to Marshall, and dropped it in there, too.

Brigit said, "OK, Mark is in the front with me, and the kids are in the back."

Brigit sat in the driver's seat, and Mark took the other front seat. Ramona was behind her Dad, and Marshall was behind Brigit.

She closed the doors and hit the seal button. The car pressurized a bit, their ears popped, and a moment later, a green light on the dash lit. "I love that popping in my ears!" Brigit said. "OK, we can go now."

"What was that?" Ramona asked.

"Well, space is a vacuum, and the car is smart enough to know if the pressure in the car is sealed and safe for humans. We are fine."

Joseph walked up and knocked on the window. She opened the door. Breaking the seal, of course.

"Can you bring this up to the moon please? It goes to Rachael Monroe, a seven-year-old living on the far side."

He handed his wife a kitten.

"I think we can do that. Are you in the kitten business now?"

"No, not a bad idea, but no. I told Rachael I would find her an orange kitten and deliver it. She said she already had the name picked out. Timing is everything." He paused momentarily, "I will call her Mom to let her know you are bringing her a kitten."

"Monroe, is that…"

"It is. The General's former and retired Boss. She wanted to talk to you about a consulting job anyway."

Brigit froze a moment. "Mark, can you run into the barn and grab one of the small, five-pound, orange bags on the table."

"Sure." He said, sounding more curious than anything else.

He returned with the bag, put it into the trunk, and closed and sealed it.

"Potassium?" He asked.

"General Monroe has a very nice garden under her dome and feeds about 40 people year-round. The problem is that the plants are wilting, and I suspect they are getting too dry. Adding potassium to the soil will help all the way around." She smiled at him, "Sometimes the gift is an asset. Sometimes, it makes me guess. This time, I saw exactly what I, or rather she, needed."

Mark smiled. He completely understood, as did Ramona. "Marshall," Brigit asked, "Do you have a gift?"

"I do, in a way. I know things about people, like if they are sincere, telling the truth, or trying to get something over on me or someone else."

Jon walked out of the house and heard the conversation. "You're a lie detector."

Marshall nodded to him.

"You and Gayle have a lot in common. She has that ability, but it is not as clear-cut. She hears thoughts – mind reading a bit, but she explains it like if you are thinking something, she can hear what you are thinking. So, if she asks you a question, you may as well answer honestly because she already heard the real answer you were thinking."

"OK, all loaded. Let's head to the station and visit the gang; I think they have lunch planned after a tour. Then, to the moon for a day of interesting fun. Besides, I must deliver a kitten to a young lady and fix her Mom's garden."

~~~~~~~~~~~~

It took another hour, but everyone was finally ready in their seat. Joseph ran out of the house, yelling as Brigit started the car after handing the kitten to Mark.

She shut it off again, and he ran up to her side. She opened the door.

"I forgot to kiss you goodbye."

Ramona said, "Awwwwwww."

Marshall and Mark laughed.

Joseph backed up a step, and she restarted the car. Mark and the others figured they needed to get moving before they could fly up, but the grav engine made them all jump as the car went straight up.

It hovered, and they could see everything. The town, both farms, the neighbors.

"Denver ground control, this is Brigit Markz in car 324."

"Hi, Brigit. Where are you heading?"

"Well, I have three tourists, and we are heading to Station 4, Magda's Place."

"Ah, visiting the boss?"

"More or less. Tour, lunch, then a trip to the moon and home by midnight."

"Tom will be on at that time. Make sure you wish him a happy birthday if you get back after midnight; tomorrow is his 40th."

"I will definitely do that. Thanks, Marcel. How's the family?"

"Doing great. Chuck has a new job, freight to and from the stations. The kids are in 4th grade now. They are getting old. Does that mean I'm getting old?"

"Not in the least. They will keep you far from getting old. Tell Chuck I said hello."

"OK, you are clear for orbital entry and straight to Station 4, Magda's Place. I figure you already have a parking spot."

"I do. Thanks. This is Brigit Markz departing the surface, 4 souls on board, heading to Station 4 directly."

"Roger that, Brigit. Four Souls posted. Good flight," a pause, "Control out."

"Affirmative Control. Brigit Markz in car 324 out."

"You all ready?"

They all nodded. She hit the thruster and pointed the car up. It jumped and pressed them all into the back of their seats.

"I love this part," Brigit said, "Getting squished into my seat." There was silence in the car.

~~~~~~~~~~~~

"Station 4, this is Brigit Markz. My garage open?"

"Yep, sure is. The bay is empty, and the airlock is open."

"Thanks, Virginia. Be there in a minute."

"I'll hop in there when the bay is green. See you in a few!" Virginia said and disconnected the comm.

Brigit flew perfectly into the bay and landed on HER spot. It was actually the closest spot to Virginia's tool area. Once she touched down, she sent the signal to the bay doors, and they closed. A moment later, the light above the door in the car and the airlock on the bay turned green.

"BRIGIT! Long time no see!"

"I know. Thought I would drop in with a few tourists. I hear you are giving us a ride to the moon, and you get to stay and play, too?"

"I do!" She saluted Brigit, "Just got my orders. Chauffer duty is always fun." She looked at the three, "Anyone want to ride up front with me?"

"Mark, you need to sit in the co-pilot seat," Brigit said.

Virginia smiled, "I may even let you fly a little?"

"Wonderful! I hear there is a lunch planned. Is it in the normal place?"

"It is. You have a couple hours. The boss is at a conference and has asked me to let you know. I can give you a tour of the station or do a little maintenance on the car?"

"I can walk them around the station, maybe the float room; how long will the mechanic stuff take?"

"Half an hour or so. Go wander aimlessly. I get to play with an antique, and for me, THIS is fun!"

Brigit messaged Magda that they had arrived and she was about to walk them around the station. She knew about the lunch and would see her in a couple of hours.

"Oh, V. Can you look after something for me while we are here?"

"Sure thing." Brigit handed her the kitten, who crawled into her neck and started purring, "Got just the place for this little darling to nap."

Brigit handed her a small container, "What's this?" Virginia asked.

"Some Joan Juice for Fuzzy." Everyone laughed, and Virginia said, "I'll get it into the cooler."

She walked to her huge toolbox and opened a drawer of rags. She laid the kitten, who curled up and fell asleep, purring gently. She put the container of milk into the wall cooler for safekeeping.

Brigit looked at her comm, and Magda messaged her reply. It was **excellent**.

"This is wild!" Ramona said.

Marshall and Mark just nodded. They were all just taking it in and trying not to look scared at the possibility of dying in the vacuum of space.

Virginia went to work on her hobby, Brigit's car. It was old. Older than anything currently flying. The Antique Society of Denver caught wind of the car, nearly 60 years old and still flying, and did a story on it.

They thought it was Virginia's car, and they let them believe that it was true, to a point. Virginia told them that the car's owner is a personal friend and that she gets to use it when it is available and does all the maintenance and restoration.

Virginia even got to drive it in an antique car parade, and once she stopped and parked, she had more people talking to her than to just about any other car parked in the lot. Most of the other drivers even stopped to talk to her. She had become a celebrity.

The four walked out of the airlock and resealed it. They went straight to the station's center, zero-G, to let them play.

"Hold on to the rails, please. We are beginning to lose gravity."

Marshall asked, "How are we losing gravity? For that matter, how is there gravity up here at all?"

Brigit knew this answer, "The station has a rotating outer hub, and at the outer edge, the wall itself, is where we landed. That outer wall is the floor, and we are moving up a ladder; the higher we get, the less effect gravity will have on us. Once in the center hub, we will experience zero gravity and fly around the room like a bird."

She paused at the door and grabbed four gas canisters. "OK, this is a gas canister. It has just air in it. If you find yourself stuck in the middle of the room, for example, hold it in your hand, with the red port facing opposite where you want to go and press the button. It clips to your belt or jacket in the meantime."

They all nodded and accepted the baseball-sized device.

Brigit opened the doorway after looking in the viewport to make sure no one was careening toward them.

"Follow my lead." She said.

Putting her hands on either side of the doorway, she pushed off and headed to the other side of the space. "Hi, Brigit?"

Brigit flipped over and saw a familiar face, "Hi, Gretchen. Relaxing a little after shift?"

"I find it more relaxing than swimming or the sauna," Gretchen said. "I see you found a few newbies?"

"These are my cousins. Mark, and his daughter Ramona, and her husband, Marshall."

"OK, welcome to Zero Space!"

They spent more than an hour in the room, got the hang of it, and Marshall used the gas ball, as he called it, to shoot around the room. Accelerating halfway and turning it around to slow to a soft landing. He figured it out quickly.

CHAPTER FIVE

Leaving the room, they placed the balls in the holder, which autorotated and lined up to mate the refill port. The balls replenished themselves with air.

"Time for lunch."

They climbed down the ladder and made it to the outer wall. It took them a minute to get their legs back.

They stood there and waited for a minute or two. Brigit walked off, and the others followed. Magda and Rory sat at a large table in a conference room with a few food trays.

Magda pointed to the seats, and they sat. Magda looked at Rory and nodded. The screens in the room were all lit, and after a minute, the three understood what they were looking at.

"That's my house," Ramona said.

"Mine too!" Brigit said, half laughing.

Mark, obviously the voice of reason on the council, asked, "OK, why are you showing this to us?"

"We, as in the people you already know, know quite a bit about your community. There are 473 people from very young to old. Living in 213 buildings. As for animals, we also see that number and where they are at any moment. We can tell you the temperature outside and inside of your home, when people wander into the hills to hunt or gather, and where the animals are they are looking for. None of us have the gift. We use technology. But, our technology is limited to the now." She looked at Brigit, Ramona, and Mark in that order, "Where-as some of you know things that either have not happened or can be avoided. Others can talk to people who have died and, as I heard, have not yet moved on."

Mark said, "I'm asking you again: Why are you showing this to us?"

Magda looked at Brigit, "I like him!" She turned to Mark and stared directly into his eyes like she was drilling a hole through the back of his head, "Because if we can find you, others can also."

Magda got quiet, and Brigit said, "Magda, you are about to propose a collaboration between you and me, between the community and the universe."

Magda grinned, "I was, am. And I was going to use those exact words also."

Ramona added, "So, camping out near the cave and waiting for the team to investigate, is that in the plan?"

"Damn. You're killing my Mojo!" Brigit nearly started laughing. "You people know how to kill a good…. Well, anyway. Let's eat. We can talk and eat."

During lunch, they planned the intervention trip to the cave. Magda, her team, and the council would come to the cave to meet with the new team. The three groups would discuss who they are, what they are, and where they live. According to Mark, this would work, leaving the settlement alone. But only for a few years.

As the planet gets smaller, regular citizens will discover the community and bring bad vibes, as

Ramona called them, to the community, and the way of life will be lost.

Brigit added that the people here need to meet with the people there. Not who they are, but that they are friends, with items to trade and information to share. Slowly bringing them into the future and not disrupting the life they all enjoy.

Virginia never made it to lunch. She sent Brigit a note that she had to finish a project with her car so she could fly home.

After informing Marissa about the events, they decided that the four would return to the council, and the entire council would travel to the cave. Brigit, Joseph, Magda, and her team would meet at the cave. Mark knew the season was approaching. The first snowfall is when the investigation team arrives at the cave.

The first snow is soon.

~~~~~~~~~~~~

The trip to the lunar surface was breathtaking. Mark sat up front with Virginia and managed to fly a little. On the Moon, Mark and Marshall donned a suit and walked on the surface. While the guys walked on the surface, Virginia, Ramona, and Brigit carried the kitten to the far side. She brought the potassium in a small messenger bag that Ramona wore. At the station, Virginia left to visit friends in the dome and would meet them back at the train in a few hours. Ramona and Brigit took the train to the far side to give a little girl a kitten and fix a field.

The transport tube went from dome to dome, like a train, and General Monroe was waiting for her on the station's platform.

Victoria saw the kitten and knew her daughter would be thrilled. It was a short walk to her home, and Ramona was introduced as her niece.

The kitten slept quietly in Brigit's arms and was nearly invisible. They walked in and sat on a very comfortable sofa. About that time, Rachael walked into the room and said hello. The kitten immediately woke as she heard the little girl's voice.

"Is that my kitty?" She asked, "Is that my Punkin?"

"Not sure, some guy gave it to me and said the owner would know it is for her. Now, what was his name?"

"Mr. Joe. His name is Mr. Joe!" She exclaimed.

"I think that is right, but the new owner has a beautiful name. What did Mr. Joe tell me?"

"RACHAEL! The little kitty is for Rachael Monroe of 1471 Rock Street, Dome 7, Far Side, Moon. THAT'S ME!" She had a smile that would not stop.

"Oh my gosh, I believe you are correct. Ramona, is that the name?"

"Yes, Aunt Brigit. That is the name Uncle Joe said – the person who needs to take really good care of this kitten."

Brigit handed the kitten to Rachael, and the kitten just knew this was her new best friend. She snuggled up to Rachael's neck, and the purr motor started. Loud and impressive.

Rachael carried her new best friend to her room, and the adults smiled. Mom had a little tear.

"SO," Brigit said, "You had a question for me?"

"I do."

Victoria stood, the others followed, and they walked out a sliding door. The garden was impressive. Corn, lima beans, tomatoes, bell peppers, jalapenos, lettuce, cabbage, and other surface plants. She looked off to one side and recognized potatoes, sweet and russett.

"Brigit," She said, "The crops are not doing well. There is something wrong. They are lifeless, wilted, and the fruit is lackluster."

Brigit walked over to a corn stalk and picked off an ear of corn. She peeled it back and looked at the kernels. Mostly normal. The leaves, however, had purple stripes. She pulled off a single kernel and tasted it. Too sweet, she thought to herself.

"General," Brigit said.

"Victoria, please."

Brigit smiled, "Victoria. Your crop has a serious issue, but we can fix it." She looked at Ramona, "This is phosphorus. A few tablespoons in a bucket, and poured in your irrigator, will fix the plants in a week or so."

Victoria smiled, "You just so happen to have that with you?"

"Yes. I had a feeling from the description of what it might be, and as it turns out, in this case, I was right. I like it when I guess correctly."

They spent a few more hours and had a small meal with Victoria and Rachael. She had no husband, and they had a great time talking. Brigit and Ramona had never heard of it before, but it was good. Brigit asked for the recipe, and Victoria messaged her.

The growing season here is as long as this side of the moon faces the sun. That is about half a month. Above the plants, Ramona noticed the lamps. So they can shed some light on the fields when they are opposite the sun.

As they were leaving, Rachael came to hug them and thank them again for the kitty.

Ramona asked, "Does the kitty have a name?"

"Yep!" She said, "Punkin. She is orange."

"Pumpkin, I love that name." When Brigit said the name, the cat looked at her, "I guess she does too!" They all laughed at the fact the cat knew its name already.

"I told Mr. Joe I wanted an orange cat to call her punkin'."

Ramona and Brigit looked at each other. Joseph must have told the cat that Pumpkin was her name, and when someone says Pumpkin, they are talking about her.

Ramona said, "We need to head back to the port. Take care of that little pumpkin."

They all said goodbye.

~~~~~~~~~~

The ride back to the spaceport was less than an hour and a half. They went through several domes and talked to many people on the train. Ramona found it interesting how many people knew Brigit. When they reached the Primary

Dome train station, they met up with Virginia and had a late dinner.

"So, what are you hungry for?" Virginia asked.

"Not sure?" Brigit and Ramona said, "Had a snack at the general's place a bit ago."

Virginia said, "How about Thai. I love Thai food."

"What's that?" Ramona asked Brigit. She waited for a reply because you could see it on her face. She had no idea.

"Lots of vegetables. A little meat. Tons of flavor and spicy!" Virginia said.

"I do like spicy," Brigit said.

They walked to the restaurant. As they entered, the aromas filled their heads. This is interesting. Virginia walked up to the counter and ordered Pad Thai, Medium Spicy.

Brigit and Ramona had no clue what the items on the menu were, so they said the same thing, only on the mild side.

They all got drinks, tea, of course. Unsweet tea mixed with a bit of lemonade. Puts the sweetness just above unsweet, and you get the full tea flavor. All three of them ordered a drink.

They sat at a table in the center of the room, and Virginia put a number in the middle of the table, 42. A few minutes later, the food arrived, and the server asked, "Medium Spicy!"

Virginia raised her hand. He dropped the recyclable tray in front of her and put the other two before Brigit and Ramona.

He placed a fork, chopsticks, and their drinks on the table. Walked away and returned a moment later with a short stack of napkins.

"Well," Virginia said, "Dig in!" She picked up her chopsticks and started eating. Brigit had seen them used but had no clue how to use them. She picked up the fork, as did Ramona.

As they ate, their eyes got wide. It had a little heat, but the unique flavors were incredible. They ate, pretty much, in silence. They were all a lot hungrier than they thought they were, or this was delicious food.

"So, what happened at the General's place?" Virginia asked.

"A little girl has a new best friend, Pumpkin," Ramona said.

"The General's plants should be good in a few days, maybe a week," Brigit ate her meal. After swallowing it, she said, "She invited us for dinner, but it was a small meal, and I was not very hungry at the moment."

Virginia asked, "What did she serve?"

"I can't remember what she called them, but they were lamb tacos with the best cucumber sauce I ever had. The tortilla was different but good."

Virginia nearly choked from laughing, "They are called Gyro's, pronounced Hero's, but spelled with a G. Oh, the tortilla is called a pita."

Ramona nearly covered them with food when she said, "That's it. That's what they were. Hear-ro's."

"We need to trip to Greece. You need to eat a REAL gyro," Virginia said.

"Girls trip. If not this collection, the next one. My car can fit five. Us three, Rory, Gayle?"

"My car can fit a lot more," Virginia said. They all laughed and continued eating.

Virginia had been to Pad Thai a lot. She used to work nearby. She gave Ramona and Brigit a tour of the dome, including the entertainment dome. They ran across Mark, who was napping on a chair.

"Dad! Wake up." Ramona said.

He opened an eye, "What? I am more comfortable than I have ever been taking a nap."

"Did you eat?" Brigit asked.

"I did. Had something called Pad Thai." The three women all laughed. "What?"

"We had the same thing. I liked it," Ramona said. "Did you leave Marshall outside?"

"No, dear. He is taking something called a first-timers tour."

Virginia said, "I used to do those. They are interesting and show you a lot of the dome and complex. Takes a couple hours. These two got a condensed version of it. Any idea when it started?"

"About 1800, I think," Mark said.

Virginia looked at the wall. The current time is visible above almost every door in this complex. "Well, 2040, he should be done by now." She walked to a wall comm, "Computer, announce Marshall Ramsey to pick up the white courtesy comm."

A few seconds later, they heard the announcement over all audio on the dome. A second later, "Hi Marshall! Where are you?" The conversation was a private comm, using an earpiece.

She disconnected and walked back to the group. She was laughing or trying not to laugh so hard that she was almost in tears.

"He is at the Thai restaurant. He's waiting for his Pad Thai to be delivered to his table." Everyone started laughing, "I said we would meet him there."

They all stood and walked back to the Thai restaurant.

~~~~~~~~~~~

They were sightseeing after leaving the restaurant, and Virginia gave them an excellent tour. One of the guides happened to pass by and stared at her.

"Virginia?" He said.

She turned and looked at him, "Michael! How are you?"

"Great. I am still here to give the tour you taught me. What are you up to?"

"I work for General Rochavarro; I lead an inspection team."

He looked at her shirt, "WO3, damn. You went from Staff Sergeant to WO?"

"In a way, I guess," She looked at Ramona and Brigit and saw Ramona frozen.

A second later, "V, we need to run. You're here a lot. Maybe you can meet and catch up next week when you return here," Ramona said.

They said their goodbyes, and as they walked off, "OK, miss, I See Things, what did you see?" Virginia asked Ramona.

Ramona smiled, "You two will have a thing. Meet him for coffee next week and let it happen."

"A thing, as in a lifetime thing?"

"All I can tell you is you are meant to be together in the next several years. I am not sure how permanent it is. However, you are happy when you are together."

Virginia looked at her, "Clear as mud, thanks."

They reached the docking area where the ship was located and prepared to head home.

Over the loudspeaker, "Would the pilot of shuttle 461 please come to the control center?"

"Be right back," Virginia said.

The others just stood there and looked around.

Virginia returned a few minutes later, "They wanted me to bring a delivery to the station. I said yes, so they are loading it now. All I know is that it is a box for the Colonel. He ordered something from a graphic store on the Moon. Pretty big box, too."

Brigit helped with the preflight, and the launch and flight were uneventful.

"Ship, call Colonel Spencer." He answered.

"What's Up, V?"

"Before we left the Moon, they asked me to bring a large box to the station. It's for you."

"Wonderful, they finished a week early," He said, "Leave it in the ship, and I'll get it myself."

"No problem. But, what is it?"

"I will tell you, come to my office on Monday morning." They disconnected.

"Cryptic?" Everyone nodded.

~~~~~~~~~~

They approached the station to park the ship and get into the car for the flight home. Virginia had the chance to upgrade a few simple things while they were floating around. She replaced the heat shielding with a newer version, making it look like the original. Hitting the atmosphere on the way home will make for an exciting adventure, as none of the others with her had ever done that.

Brigit spoke into the air, "Ship, call Magda."

"What's up?" Magda asked.

"About ready to park."

"Well, I am not there at the moment."

"Where are you?"

"I am about to park and meet with the officer in charge of the mapping. I'll drop in this evening for dinner."

"Understood. Bring the wine!" Brigit smiled at the Chief.

After the call disconnected, "That is rather odd." Virginia said.

"It is," Brigit replied. She closed her eyes to see if anything would appear in her mind. She saw the station, the room where the meeting was about to happen, and then part of the discussion regarding the mapping.

"Evidently, the mapping and identification of the settlement have already taken place, and they have a team planning to visit the settlement by air in a couple weeks." She paused momentarily, "Rory's friend saw the community, and as he should, he reported it to his superiors. When he visits the farm, he will travel with us to the cave to hold off the invasion and leave the community as alone as possible." She paused again, "Magda talks to the General in command of the mapping operation and lays out who we are and what we are. He agrees to leave us alone but wants to meet with the community leadership. We will meet at the cave, and while there, we will get the first snow."

Virginia asked, "So, all is good?"

"More or less. It's still not a done deal, but the community seems to be left alone for now. I am worried; I had another vision a few weeks ago where cars landed in the square, and no one seemed to pay them much attention. I wish I had an idea when that was. Those in the square, I did not recognize the community members. But if I had to guess, it was about 15 years from now."

Mark asked, "Why 15 years?"

"I planted that tree, a Douglas Fir, near the bench in the town center. It was quite large in the vision and is likely not all that big now."

"I know that tree," Marshall said, "Maybe nine feet tall at the moment."

"In the vision, it is closer to 25 feet, maybe a little more. So, I think the community will join the universe in the next decade. Because I did not know those in the square, it can mean that they were very young when I knew them or were not born in the community."

"Strange thought." Ramona and Marshall said together.

"OK." Virginia said, "Who needs to be at the cave?"

They talked for a few more minutes while Virginia parked and walked the group to the car. They all sat in their places, and Brigit waved to the Chief as she did her preflight. Virginia left through the airlock and secured the door.

"All safe here!" She said through the com.

"Thanks, V. See you at dinner," she said. She looked at the clock: 2357.

The garage door opened, and Brigit maneuvered through it to open space.

"Station Control, this is Brigit Markz departing the garage."

"Heading home?"

"I am. Got a few tourists with me and planning to test the new heat shielding."

"That is gonna be pretty!" There was a pause, "You are cleared for direct approach to the Denver space. Note departure is at 2358."

"Thanks, Will. I'll be getting on Ground Control in a moment."

"Have a nice flight, Brigit. Station Control out."

"Brigit Markz out and switching to Denver ground." She floated the car for a few minutes and saw the West Coast approaching them. She pressed a few buttons, "Denver ground, this is Brigit Markz."

"Hi, Brigit. You are cleared to enter the atmosphere and hold a few moments over Colorado Springs. Got a heavy in front of you with a little hydraulics issue."

"Understood, Tom, and by the way, HAPPY BIRTHDAY!"

"OK, how did you know?"

"A little bird told me when I left this morning."

"Is that little bird's name Marcel?"

"Maybe!"

"Hey, just got a note you are requesting to do a flare. Stand by a sec."

Tom came back, "OK. Flare approved, watch your speed and vector, and have fun. Drop over Colorado Springs and maintain 3,000 feet. Head due north. You know where you live."

"I do, thanks." She paused, "Have a good birthday."

"Denver ground out. You are cleared to proceed."

"Brigit Markz out."

Brigit floated the car over the United States but maintained her position until she was cleared to land, or rather, she entered the atmosphere over Colorado Springs and had a low approach to the house.

"Aunt Brigit, what's a flare?" Ramona asked.

"You are about to experience something that Chief R did the first time we flew in this car. You ready?"

Everyone said no at the same time.

"OK, wonderful! Hang on!"

Mark asked, "To what!!"

She pointed the car toward the Earth and hit the engine. The acceleration even shocked her till she remembered Virginia was tinkering. As she kissed the outer atmosphere, she hit the retro and flared, bringing the nose up. Flame, or rather plasma, rolled past the windows. The tourists were all screaming, but they were all smiling.

~~~~~~~~~~

With the car parked, the four exited the garage and headed to the Janning's house. Walking through the path they cut in the hedge, they saw Jon standing on the porch. He had a cup in his hand, so it must be tea, decaf tea, this late or, more accurately, early morning.

"Howdy, kids, nice night. Not a single cloud in the sky. Perfect night for a flare." He said it nonchalantly; they all froze as they started up the steps.

"You saw that?" Mark asked.

"I did. It was spectacular, by the way."

"How did you know?" Ramona asked.

Jon tapped his head with his index finger, "I used my kidney," He chuckled a second, "The station called me to say it should be gorgeous since the sky was so clear. He suggested I vid the entire thing."

Marshall asked, "Did you?"

"Did I what?" Jon asked, grinning.

"Did you get the event recorded?"

"Of course I did. Wanna see?"

All four yelled, "YES!"

They went inside, and Jon already had it queued up on the screen.

They watched it a dozen times and loved it.

CHAPTER
SIX

Leaving the house and heading for the barn, the four travelers headed home in an hour or so. Magda walked through the hedge and surprised Ramona.

She entered the garage and looked at the four, "Got a question. What would be the repercussions if Brigit and Joseph were to walk into the community?"

Mark thought momentarily, "Well, they would wonder how they survived first off, then why it took them four years to get home. There would be a lot of questions, but ultimately, not all that much."

Marshall took over the speaking role, "As the truth seeker, and well known in the community as such, if I believed them and their story, the rest of the community would take it in stride."

Ramona added, "So, your answer is not all that much."

"Is there an end to this means?" Marshall asked.

"Not really, just gathering data," Magda said. She left, stopped, and turned to face Ramona, "Ramona, can you bring your daughter to the cave. I would love to meet her, and since she already knows the score, she may as well be in the game." She grinned, "She does understand the concept of keeping a secret?"

"She does, and I will bring her."

"Well, I need to head to the office. Have a good trip." She reached into her pocket and tossed Mark a small device.

"What's this?" He asked.

"It is an infrared strobe. When you leave the community, twist it to turn it on and put it somewhere on the cart that can be seen from above. We will see you depart the community and meet you at the cave."

"Kinda obvious it is not ours," Ramona said. Mark handed it to her, "It looks like a rock."

Magda took out her comm and switched on the camera. She faced it at the walls, ceiling, and finally, the rock. "Beyond human visual range, the camera can see it like a bonfire."

Ramona smiled and put it into her pocket. Magda pointed the camera at her pocket, and it glowed. She removed and twisted it the other way, and it shut off.

Marshall said, "Serena did ask that we bring her the glowing rock from our trip."

"You're right. I guess her gift is pretty strong already." Mark said.

As she left the barn, Magda said, "I'll have the Chiefs pick up some kid-size warm clothing before we arrive. They love shopping. How big is she?"

Ramona put her hand, palm facing down, just below her breasts.

"Perfect, thanks."

Ramona returned to the house, and Mark and Marshall tied the items on the cart down. The weather was expected to be nice but cold. The Magda gear will be welcome when they get to the cabin and the cave.

As Ramona entered the house, Brigit and a woman she did not know were on the vid.

"So, we checked for worms and discovered that we have worms. Good call. They are little buggers too. Never would have seen them if we weren't looking for them," the unknown woman said.

"Wonderful, Melinda. What's your plan to get rid of them?"

"That's the easy part. Highly susceptible to UV radiation. We'll clear the field and light it up for an hour after soaking the dirt. It draws them all to the surface, then lights them up!"

"Instant compost!"

"We had that thought also."

"Can you collect a few and put them into a test tube, fill it with alcohol, and save it for me. I like my own version of research."

"Sure thing, gotta run. Tell Tommy I said hi, and he has not been here in almost three months."

From off camera, "THREE MONTHS! I'll have a little mission for him to head there for a few days and pick up Brigit's science project. He'll be there Monday for dinner."

"Thanks, General! I'll let his sister know," The vid disconnected.

Magda said, "Call Mik Spencer at the office," The call connected.

"Howdy, Boss. What's up?"

"I need a set of orders, not classified, but they need to appear they are classified. They are for Lt. Reilley. He needs to head to Mars. He is to be assigned to a department. The particulars of the assignment will be handed to him once he lands on Mars. He is to contact the bay's NCOIC." She grinned, "Get Biff in on this and tell him we will owe him a favor."

"He'll love that!" Mik said.

"He is to be on Mars for four days," She said

Brigit added, "Maybe five days?"

"May as well just make it a week," Mik joked.

The general nearly laughed, "OK, a week. Make it a TDY. The orders to Biff are to notify Tommy's sister when he is on final. He needs to look nervous at the idea of just who is in the conference room and have Biff direct Tommy to that conference room, where his confidential assignment will be divulged."

"Got it. Consider it done. When does he leave?" Mik asked.

"Monday morning after a good breakfast. Flight home is the following Monday."

"It will take about ten hours to get there in his car."

"I know. Virginia has been working on the second staff car; it should cut that in half. Tell him to take it and give it a shakedown. Wear a pressure suit during the flight, and bring a lunch."

"Got it." Mik disconnected.

"OK, now what?" Magda asked.

Gayle asked if she wanted to brush the horses.

~~~~~~~~~~~

Mik disconnected the vid from Magda and thought for a moment. Biff should be in the bay. "Office. Call Master Sergeant Robert Wellington in the bay on Mars."

It took a little longer than expected. "Sergeant Wellingt... Oh, Hi, Major! I mean, Colonel!"

"Howdy, Biff. Got a little assignment for you if you wanna have a little fun."

"Are you kidding? I like you guys. Your Weird!"

"Why thank you, Biff. So happy you noticed." Mik outlined his plan for Tommy, then said, "The general said if you do this, if you and your crew pull this off, she owes you a favor. Pretty much anything in her wheelhouse."

Biff thought for a minute, smiled a devilish grin, and then said, "There is a restaurant, a pizzeria, in the lunar dome."

"I know, right next to the Thai place."

"That's the one. There are 17 of us here at shift change. I would love to have a pizza party, and the general deliver the pizza. The rest of the crew will be in the most amazing shock. It will be fantastic!"

"Oh, dear, lord, Biff. That is spectacular! What do you want on your pizzas?"

"At least two need to be cheese for the veg heads. The rest, mix them up."

"How many vegetarians are there?"

"Four."

"Gocha!" Mik smiled, "The general will deliver your order the next time we are headed your way. I think that's next month, actually."

Mik set up the assignments and sent them to Magda for approval. She nearly cracked up. She had to share what they were up to with the others in the house, and they loved it.

~~~~~~~~~~~~

Mik arrived in his office early Monday morning and waited till Tommy signed in. "Office, contact Lieutenant Reilley and ask him to come to my office."

A few minutes later, "You need me, Colonel?"

"I do. I have an assignment for you, and you need to head to Mars to meet with a confidential informant. You'll be there working in that department for a week. Then you head back with the item you are given."

Mik handed him his orders. Tommy read them, "Sir, I get to drive the new car? Does the Chief know?"

"She does, and she has the new car set to be quite a bit faster than the car you currently are assigned. This is also its checkout ride, so wear a suit, carry an extra power cell and your lunch, and put it through its paces."

"The orders tell me to get to the bay, and my next 'phase' will be given to me."

"That is correct. It's not classified, but it's the next best thing. Head to the bay office when you get there, and you will be directed to the person giving you the phase 2 briefing."

"OK, Colonel. Sounds interesting." He left and headed to the bay.

~~~~~~~~~~~

Brigit sat at the table in her house. The coffee seemed especially good today. Joseph sat across from her, staring into her eyes, and then he noticed a blank stare being returned. He knew what that meant.

"HOUSE. Call Mik Spencer, priority connection."

Mik answered, but before he spoke, Brigit said, "Mik, where are the kids?"

"In the fast shuttle, Tommy returned last night from Mars. They are heading to the belt station to drop off clothing and other supplies. Why?"

"Who is in the left seat?"

"Virginia, Rory is giving her a check ride," Mik said, "House conference in Chief Rory Mitchel, priority connection."

A second later, "Hi all."

"Rory," Brigit said, "Do not think about this. Put your helmet on, Virginia, too. Then stand next to Virginia, as close as you can get. HURRY!"

She did, and she stood near Virginia. A minute later, a rock flew through the window and embedded itself into the console behind, or more precisely, through the seat she was sitting in.

The rock hit the camera in front of her seat, where she answered the call.

"HOLY SHIT! What the hell was that?"

Mik screamed, "Are you two OK?"

"We are, thanks to Miss Vision." She grabbed the other camera and faced it at the seat straight through.

"I believe if you look at the console behind your seat, you will find a rock made of pure titanium," Brigit said.

Rory moved the camera to the console. The rock was maybe nine inches in diameter, smooth but rough.

"Keep it. Next time you're home, bring it to my dad's store. Tell Monica what happened, not all of it, please, unless she is alone, and she will clean it up and mount it for you." Mik said.

Rory spoke, "Brigit, I owe you a LOT of drinks. Maybe dinner or my firstborn!"

Virginia said, "We will declare an emergency to get an inside berth for the ship and replace the glass. Talk to you all soon." She disconnected.

~~~~~~~~~~

"Station A3, this is Shuttle 461 on approach. We are declaring an emergency."

"Shuttle 461, identify your emergency."

"A large rock crashed through our windshield and directly through the co-pilot's seat into the console behind it. From what we can see, we require a new window, seat, and, thankfully, a storage locker door."

"Shuttle 461. Was anyone injured," Rory looked at Virginia.

"A3, this is the copilot. I was providing the check ride for the new pilot. After this, she is licensed! There were no injuries."

"Good to hear, Rory. Park inside, bay one. You are cleared for straight in approach. You'll be here a few days, so after that experience, you get a little vacation. Drinks are on me."

"Could you let our boss know? Tell her we were talking to the Colonel when it happened."

"Will do 461. See you in a minute. Control out."

"Thanks, A3. Be there shortly. By the way, I want that rock as a souvenir!" Rory said.

"I guessed you would, A3 control out."

Virginia said, "Shuttle 461, clear. Two minutes to touchdown. Open the doors, please."

The bay doors opened, and Virginia flew it in perfectly and parked it in bay one. Closest to maintenance.

Virginia said, "Bay control. Powering down. Thanks for the repairs."

"Virginia, welcome. I talked to the general. She said to give her a call after you get some food. Bay control out."

Rory said, "I guess they all know by now. Let's get this over with…." Rory took a few snapshots of the damage and sent them to everyone, including Commander Victor Zamir.

They managed to get to the galley and grab a burger and a coffee. They were sitting at the table with a terminal and placed the call. Brigit answered, and then everyone else appeared in the room. Brigits home.

"Hi, gang," Victor appeared on the screen. "You broke my ship!" He said loudly and with a smile.

"Sorry!" The Chiefs said together.

"Let's see. You are at A3. You need a window, a seat, and at least the door to the locker. Let maintenance know they will be there in a few hours. I'll send my head chief to make you a new ship."

"Victor, that is amazing," Magda said. "Chief…. Chiefs, both of you are on detached duty till you fix my ship and bring it home."

"Yes, general." They said together. They like playing maintenance!

CHAPTER SEVEN

It took under a week to fix everything, but the ship is as good as new. Several wiring harnesses needed to be removed, but the damage was not severe. If Rory had been sitting in her seat, for her, it would have been fatal.

After bringing the ship back to the station for the general, the first stop is to hug Brigit. If not for her, Rory would have been ventilated in a way a human body should not be ventilated. Virginia may have survived, but there would have been medical issues since her helmet was out of reach. She would have experienced the vacuum of space more than she wanted.

"Rory," Magda said as she grabbed and hugged Rory like a plush bear. She finally let her go, "Give her my thanks also, please, take care and go visit." She handed her a giant bottle of champagne. "Now go, give her my best and that hug I gave you."

No other words were spoken. Rory and Virginia walked to the car and did the preflight. Magda entered the airlock, secured the door, and opened the garage door. Virginia looked at the door as it opened, and the trim went from green to red. The garage was in a vacuum. The car launched and headed for the farm.

"Be safe, you two." Magda said, "I almost lost you both. That would have been…."

"General, is there something I can do for you?"

She turned away and said, "Tommy! Grab a car, and let's get to the farm. We are bringing dessert to a dinner party."

"Excellent, Ma'am. May I suggest the Cannoli Pie from Orbital Bakers?"

"Go get two. Meet me back here, and we can head down. Got an extra car?"

Tommy Reilley smiled, "Got just the thing. You'll love it!"

"Should I be scared?" Magda asked.

As he ran out of the hall and around the corner, he yelled back to her, "Well, maybe a little."

Magda smiled. She loves her team!

~~~~~~~~~~~~~~~~~

"Where in the hell did you find this thing?" Magda said.

They already entered the atmosphere and were about to ask to be cleared to land at the farm.

Magda mentioned, "Oh, Lieutenant. Are we not going just a little fast?"

"Yes, Ma'am, we are. This is great!" Tommy was cracking up, "This is the property of Virginia and Mik; it says so on the side. However, I got permission to use it in an emergency."

The car was tiny. The occupants were only two people. The second seat was behind the driver, who sat in front. It was referred to as a cigar, but although the compartment was small, the ship was the length of Brigit's car, maybe a foot longer, and less than half the width. However, it had the same engine.

Magda asked, "Between here and Mars, how long?"

Tommy thought a moment, "Maybe three hours. But there ain't enough room for wearing of a pressure suit. So, TransPo takes a dim view of traveling that far in this ship. They are more designed as hot rods. Dirt to station, maybe the Moon."

Magda laughed, "Get with me in the conference room tomorrow after breakfast. Got something for you?"

"What's that boss?"

"A new pressure suit you can wear in this little car and be comfortable."

"REALLY!!!" Tommy turned to look at Magda. She winked at him.

"They are still experimental but looking really good. Solid little suits."

"Excellent!" He contacted the ground, "Denver control, this is speeder 001."

"001, what are your intentions?" The controller said, laughing slightly.

"The general and I are heading to visit Brigit." He said it as if everyone knew Brigit.

A slight pause, "Well, let's see. You are a thousand miles from the farm, and at your speed, you better start slowing down, or you will miss Colorado," He laughed, "Actually, I see you will be at the farm in 3 minutes. Nothing in your way. Speed at your desire. Clear for straight in."

"Thanks, control. Any issue with a low-level flight over the house at, say, 3,000 feet at about 800 MPH?"

"That will let them know you are there. Stand by." About 15 seconds passed, "001. You are clear in your approach, but please do not go lower than 3,500 feet. Let's not break any windows."

"Understood, 001 out."

"Control out."

Magda did not say a word. She just sat there. On the other hand, Tommy made a beeline for the farm, and at 3,500 feet, precisely between the two houses, the sonic boom made their presence known.

He flipped over, slowed by using the main engine, and landed in front of the barn on the Jansens' property.

Virginia stood on the steps, "How's my car, Tommy?"

"Perfect, Chief!"

"OK, why are you here? What's the emergency?" Rory asked.

Magda was getting out of the little car, "We brought dessert!"

"Good enough!" Virginia said. "How did she handle?"

"Like a dream. It was almost like she was guessing what I planned to do next. You did a fantastic job."

"Tommy?" Magda said.

"Yes, boss?"

"Bring those two to breakfast, but don't let on why?"

"Yes, boss…." He laughed.

"That's not fair!" Virginia said.

Rory added, "Will we like it?"

All Tommy and Magda did was nod their heads.

The group walked into the house.

~~~~~~~~~~~

Dinner ended, and they sat with the rest of the champagne, coffee, and Cannoli Pie.

"So, Tommy. How was the classified trip to Mars?" The general asked.

"You guys scared the shit out of me. I had to get there, and in the bay office, I was told the operative I needed to meet up with was in the conference room. Biff looked scared of that thought, and I wanted to run. I opened the door, and my sister told me the Colonel set me up orders, making her my temporary supervisor for a week. I stayed at her house and had a blast." He reached into a pocket, "Here is your sample, Brigit." He handed her a sealed metal tube.

"I'll look at it tomorrow on the station in the lab. Thanks!"

"This pie is great!" Mik said.

Everyone nodded. No one spoke. They ate the pie in relative silence.

About 5 minutes later, the pie plates were empty, and Magda asked, "Brigit." All she did was look at her.

Brigit got the idea, "I saw the rock come through the window, and I saw Rory… uh…. Injured. I had no idea where they were, so I called Mik, who called Rory. She stood and put her helmet on, as did Virginia. A minute later, the rock hit the plane."

Magda smiled and held Brigit's hand, "If you ever need to tell me to do or not do something, call me!" Everyone nodded.

Gayle asked, "You all spending the night? It is about 2am already."

Virginia spoke, "I need to be at the station at 8am for a meeting regarding the new power cells. Maybe twenty minutes, but I need to be there, not virtual."

Magda said, "I have an 8am call with my boss. Let's you and I take the speeder back. The rest can take the car and get up for a 1030 brunch in the conference room. Brigit, you are invited too. I need a briefing on your little friend there," She said, pointing to the tube, "Where's Joseph?"

"New Zealand. He'll be home tomorrow afternoon," Brigit said. "I'm headed to my bed. You all staying here or at my place?"

Magda, Mik, and Virginia stayed at Gayle and Jon's.

Virginia looked out the window, "It is pouring out there. When did it start raining?"

Rory said, "So happy we can take the subway!"

Everyone cleaned up fast and headed to bed. Rory, Tommy, and Brigit opened the counter and headed to the basement for a short but very dry walk to the house.

~~~~~~~~~~

Magda and Virginia woke up early, early enough to help with chores. Brigit and Rory took care of the few items they needed to take care of and headed to Gayles. Since it was still raining, they took the underground passage and headed to the barn to see if they could help since Gayle and Jon had a lot more chores that needed to be done. As Rory said, they helped with a few things and headed into the house, running between the raindrops.

Rory said, "Don't you just love a pre-winter rain?

Magda and Virginia headed to the station in the speeder, and the first order of business was breakfast. They opted for the dining hall, standard items, but well made. They left together; Magda went to her office, and Virginia went to hers. She and Rory shared a large office off the parking garage.

There were two offices off the garage, and when Tommy made LT, they emptied the other and made it his office. He had more roles and responsibilities as an officer, so an office was a good idea, but in his mind, it was unnecessary. The funny thing is he made it look like he was in a dome office on Mars. He said he felt better looking at the mural on the wall; he knew it was fake, but Mars always made him feel better.

Mik had an office a few doors from Magda, and it looked like the Moon. His favorite place. The box they carried from the Moon a few weeks ago had his mural and items in it, which made it look as though the exterior of the office was the lunar surface.

Rory and Virginia, now their office, was rather unique. It had car and ship designs, formulas, and skin color ideas, and it looked like a ship design center. Victor, Commander Zamir, showed up one afternoon and sat in their office. When they walked in and saw him, they asked what he was doing. His reply was to get new ideas. The Chiefs grinned when he said it. They proceeded to inundate him with thoughts, improvements, and upgrades.

A few after Virginia and Magda went to their meetings, Brigit arrived in her car and parked in the garage. She was followed by Rory, carrying Mik and Tommy in the general's car.

Magda was about to enter the garage when they flew up. Once the door changed to green, she walked in, "So, why two cars?" She asked.

Brigit said, "Picking up Joseph in a couple hours and getting to New Zealand from here is easier than home."

Rory added, "I needed to get the car home.."

Mik commented, "Well, boss, I wanted to be chauffered."

Tommy didn't say a word.

"Uh huh," Magda said, grinning as Rory shook her head, standing next to Mik.

Brigit had the tube in her hand and was quiet. Everyone looked at her, and she realized everyone was looking at her, "What?' She said.

"What are you thinking?" Mik asked.

"Well," she paused a moment, "I was thinking. Suppose there is a different form of radiation that these little worms encountered on the way to Mars. It is Earth soil, and the container used, if memory serves me right, is not all that protective." She looked at Rory, "What is the speed of the hauler that carried the dirt?"

"A little slower than your car, why? What are you thinking?" Rory asked.

"I was just thinking out loud. But, since you asked, suppose the dirt was exposed to various cosmic rays that the ship protects us against. How can we verify my thought?"

Virginia said, "That's actually easy. We pull a sensor pack behind the car, get up to the hauler speed, and coast to Mars like they do. Maybe a 19-hour trip, but it is thorough."

Magda and Mik stood there and watched this interaction. This is what they each love about the team. No idea or thought is wrong, and everyone participates in a resolution to a problem.

"Brigit," Magda asked, "Are you volunteering your car for this experiment?"

"I am. Virginia can fly it, and Rory and I can follow in the shuttle. I need a few hours anyway in the left seat. Flying slow takes more practice than flying fast."

"I have a friend that owes me a favor. Let me get a sensor pack we can tow in the car." Virginia thought a moment, "I say 100 feet behind. This way, the car will not affect the sensor package."

"Keep me posted," Magda said as she walked out.

Mik started smiling; everyone just stared at him. Finally, he spoke, "OK, I promised Biff that the General would deliver pizzas from that place in the lunar dome the next time we were there, and that would be when we take our little drive to Mars towing the pack."

Brigit smiled, "Let me guess. Magda has no idea about being a pizza delivery driver."

"You guessed it."

Brigit asked, "When do you plan to tell her?"

"I'm thinking," Mik rubbed his chin, "Just before we land." He turned to the Chief, "Chief, how soon can you be ready to do this?"

"Two days." She shook her head at Mik, "What time do we need to be in the bay at Mars to provide this pizza party?"

"What pizza party?" Magda asked as she walked back into the room.

Mik came clean and told her everything.

"So boss, you up for delivering 20 pies from the Moon to Biff in the Mars bay?"

Magda looked disturbed. They all knew that look. Not upset, playful. "Definitely."

"Good. We leave in a couple days, and since the ship is a lot faster than the car, they can leave whenever, and we can catch up easily enough."

Magda said, "Office, call Pie in the Sky in the Lunar Colony." A minute later, a woman appeared on the screen.

"Pie in the… Oh, hi General, what can I do for you?"

"Need an order for two days from now. We are bringing them to Mars for a party. So, they need to stay hot."

"Bring the carriers back from Mars with you, and we can do it. How many do you need?"

Mik spoke, "There are 20 people, hungry people. 4 are vegetarian. The rest are omnivores."

"So, one plain cheese and a few veggies. Can we mix the rest up?"

"Have fun. We figured 20 large pizzas so they can all have some leftovers."

She entered a bunch into her terminal, "$400, you get the bulk order discount."

Mik said, "Make it $500, call it your tip, and you can all split it since you will all most likely be working on it," He grinned and looked at Magda, "Send the invoice to the General!"

"Really. You OK with that, General?"

She shook her head and said, "That's fine. We will be there on Thursday morning to pick them up. How long will they stay hot?"

"In the heat boxes, let's see. Five heat boxes with four pies each, so one can be the veggie-only box. You should be good for about 18 hours at just below oven temp."

"Only need about eight, so we're good."

"OK, Colonel. How long is the trip?"

"About 5 hours, and they must be on Mars at 4pm. So, if we need to be there at 4, minus 5 hours….." Mik grinned at her.

"I got an idea. How about picking the pizzas up at, say, 11am," She laughed while she said it.

"Perfect, you're good. The computer came up with the same timeline!"

"OK, see you Thursday at 11. They will be in the boxes and ready to deliver." She waved to Mik, who waved back, and she disconnected.

Magda told the group, "Chief V! This is your baby. Tell everyone what they are doing."

Virginia thought a moment and grabbed a portapadd. After a few minutes, she looked at the group.

"OK, the way I see it, there are two pilots and two copilots. Colonel, you and Rory are in the car pulling the pack. Brigit, you are piloting the shuttle to Mars with a pizza stop on the moon. The Lieutenant is flying the right seat. General, you and I will monitor the instrument pack in the back."

Mik spoke, "What's your logic for the assignments?"

Virginia almost second-guessed herself at the question, then said, "Our most experienced flight team is in the most hazardous position. Pulling the pack makes the vehicle less stable, and experience will be needed to get there in one piece. Brigit needs a few more hours in the left seat to be fully licensed, and I can validate her time in the left seat. Tommy, well, that is the only craft he is not 100% certified on, so I figure if he sat in the right seat, it would give him familiarity with the operation and flight characteristics, and if I know Brigit, she will give him the once over. He will get a little flight time himself. He will be certified in a month between Rory and the Colonel." She looked at Magda, "I will be watching the screen in the event of a sensor pop, and I put the boss with me because she sees things others miss."

Mik grinned, "PERFECT!" He added, "Who launches when?"

"The way I see it, it is about a 10-hour flight in the car if it maintains the same speed as the dirt hauler, So stay around 6,000 miles per second to give it a little leeway. I say they launch at about 0600. Then, at 1100, Brigit must be at the Moon to pick up the pizzas. She can catch up to the car easily, and I recommend staying 1,000 miles off port-aft and a little lower to give a clear view. The sun and the belt should be around the starboard aft for maximum effect on the sensor pack."

Magda said, "Excellent. Do it!" and left the room.

Rory stood and said, "I need to run to visit Mrs. Colonel. She needs to mount a rock for me." She pulled the nearly ten pounds of pure titanium from a bag she had at her feet and handed it to Mik.

"That thing is pretty. It should look amazing after Monica fixes it all up."

"I was thinking the same thing." She put the rock back into the bag, slung it over her shoulder, and headed to the public transport pad.

Mik yelled, "You can always take the little car?"

She left the room and said, "Naw, ain't been on the bus in a while."

~~~~~~~~~~~

Everyone was thrilled that the timeline had a little breathing room built in. It seems that hanging a 300-pound sensor pack off the back of a small ship creates a unique set of variables.

They picked up the pack on the moon, so they all stayed the night and departed for Mars from the station in orbit. Victor helped with a retro-pack on the leading edge of the sensor array. He keyed it to auto-fire if the tension on the cable dropped below 100 pounds. This way, it will maintain a taught cable on its own throughout the flight to Mars. The rocket engines' firing creates chaos in the car's direction, so Rory and Mik need to watch it closely.

Rory asked, "Colonel, will Monica be joining us on Mars? She can fly with Brigit."

"No, Monica has taken over the store full-time since my Dad passed. She is looking for a buyer, someone who will be acquiring not only the shop but the mineral rights in the section of the belt he owned; I guess we own it all at the moment." He started rambling a little, "Kind of odd that Dad is gone, but then to discover he was one of the wealthiest men in the system, well, just odd. He never let on. Since Mon and I are now the owners, we are set for life. Why am I still doing this?" He paused, "If we find someone who wants it and is willing to pay the price for everything, the whole kit and caboodle, we talked about it and will let it go for their first offer with one stipulation. They need to operate it for at least ten years, and as our new friends say, they need to do it to help humanity." He winked at Rory, "Ever thought about geology, metallurgy, blacksmithing?"

Rory smiled, "First off, NOPE! Never thought about it. Second, you are doing this because you love it! It is definitely not for the pay."

"True." He said.

"However, does the boss know how rich you are?" She said, smiling.

"Yes and no. How do you think I can pick up all these cars and speeders for V to play with. Don't tell her any of this, please. But on her birthday, I am gifting her a 26 Luxury Lunar. Roomy, slow, but the best thing that can fly."

"Holy shit, she's going to explode. She's been hoping one day to just touch one."

"I know. I ran across it on Mars about four months ago, and the owner got it flying. I brought it to Victor and his crew; they have been restoring it and are almost finished. Her birthday is in a few weeks. I can give you a TDY for the last week, and you can head there and help out, then fly it to the station and park it in her garage. We can say it is from the two of us."

"You sure?"

"I am."

"Then I agree."

"I'll let the General in on this; she can cut orders for you. Now, let's get into position. We launch in a few minutes. Did you bring lunch?"

CHAPTER EIGHT

"Lunar control to car…. Hey, is that Brigit's car?"

"It is," Rory replied.

"Does she know you two hot shots are playing in her car?" The controller, a friend of all, laughed as she said it.

"Yes, Margy, she knows. We need something slow to complete an experiment, and her little classic car fits the bill perfectly."

"OK, kid. Just be nice."

"OK, Margy. We are the nicest people in the system." She paused momentarily, "Control, this is Car 324, leaving lunar orbit at Station Zed.

The destination is Mars. A slow leisurely trip estimating about ten hours."

"Who's with you?"

Mik touched his microphone, "It's me, Margy, Mik. I'm in the right seat today."

"Colonel, in the right seat? AH! Vacation. Got it. You can get there faster than that, you know?"

"We know. But for this experiment, we need to be at the speed of a dirt hauler."

"Understood."

"Control, car 324 departing lunar orbit for Mars, two souls on board. We will have a sensor pack in tow and traveling at a speed of around 6k per second. Our shuttle will depart lunar space and catch up to us in a few hours, and we will all land on Mars at about 1600 hours."

"Understood 324. Safe journey. I guess you know the way. Nothing in your way."

"Car 324 out."

"Lunar control out."

Rory spoke, "Car, call Magda."

"Magda?" Mik said, chuckling a little.

"It's Brigit's car. She has the general keyed as Magda, not the general."

Magda appeared on the screen in front of them, "Hi kids, you off?"

"We are. See you in a few hours, " Mik said.

"Boss, I'll send our transponder in case Brigit does not have it memorized. This way, you can find us easier."

"Gocha! Safe flight. See you in about six hours. We will fly the last couple of hours with you."

"Roger that!" They disconnected.

"Car, call Master Sergeant Wellington at Mars base," Mik said.

"Master serg…. Oh, Hi, Colonel! I take it that means…."

"Yes, it does."

"Need assistance carrying the packages?" Biff asked.

"We do, there are 5 packages, hot boxes."

"How about I put a grav cart next to bay 14. You can offload them and put them in the cart. Who's flying, and what?"

"Rory and I are in Brigit's car, but the general's shuttle has your cargo, and Brigit Markz is the pilot."

"Wow, licensed already? She is a go-getter!"

"Actually, this is her final check flight. The general plans to hand her the cert in the bay after we drop off the delivery."

Biff replied, "That's a great idea. Bay 14 will also test her landing, taxi, and parking skills!"

"Excellent. See you at about 1600. I'll call when we hit Mars space to let you know."

The call disconnected, and they got to work.

"Rory, are we at nominal speed?"

"Yep."

"OK, releasing the clamps, extending tether."

As the winch released to 100 feet, the action of the winch stopping pulled the sensor pack back toward the car. Rory sped up ever so slightly, and the cable extended again. Before they hit full length, Mik kicked on the auto-stabilizing retro engines they installed on the sensor pack, and it pulled on the cable, throwing the car into a positive Z-axis pitch.

"DAMN! When the rockets took over, the car pulled up. This may be some work."

"Should have made the winch mount point much lower, like on the trunk or the lower rear of the frame."

"But as it is, on the rear edge of the roof, the pack lands on the trunk and is secure for landing," Rory said, then added, "Between us, we can make it work." She looked at the dashboard.

"Uh…." Mik said, looking at the display.

"Yeah, I see it too." Rory pushed the nose down and pulled it to the left.

Mik smiled, "On the beam." He winked at her, "Now keep it there, Chief!"

"Yes, sir!" She smiled back.

Rory looked at the time, "Excellent, only nine and a half hours left, and I'm already hungry."

Mik reached into the back seat, "Here you go." He handed her a paper-wrapped thing.

Rory unwrapped it, "Cheese and egg biscuit with sausage. Perfect! Now all I need is…."

"….a cup of coffee," Mik finished the sentence as he handed her a zero-G cup how she liked it. They flew, ate, and had a nice conversation. It's been a while since they just sat and talked between worlds.

~~~~~~~~~~

At about 1pm, Brigit, Magda, and Virginia entered the Pie in the Sky pizzeria. Tommy was on the ship doing the preflight.

"GENERAL! Perfect timing." She pointed to a few hot boxes.

"Those must be the hot boxes?" Virginia said. "Glad we changed the time. Our schedule changed. Thanks for adapting."

Brigit added, "Well, it has HOT BOXES stenciled on the sides."

They all laughed.

"OK. We can drop the boxes off on the way home."

A man and woman came out of the back room, the kitchen, "If it is not too much trouble. There is a bakery under the dome – a coffee house, more or less. Can you bring a few of the cookies they make? They are the best cookies we have ever eaten."

"They are!" Brigit said, "You will have those cookies when we return the hot boxes."

They collected the boxes, and Magda's comm went off, "Hello?"

"My wife with you?" Joseph asked.

"Hello to you too, Joseph. Where are you?"

"Just landed on the Moon before heading home. I need a ride."

"Meet us at bay 4, and we can give you a lift. We have one stop first, but you can ride with us."

"OK…" Before he finished asking where the stop was, Magda disconnected. Virginia and Brigit looked at Magda, "We really do have one stop before heading home. Mars is not exactly on the path to the house, but I told him the truth!" She started laughing like a maniacal scientist.

They walked and made their way to the port, passing through outgoing since they had their own ship, which was easy. Joseph was waiting at the steps and carried some hot boxes into the ship for them.

The ship loaded, secured, and pressurized, and Brigit, sitting in the left seat, launched.

"So, where are you bringing all these pizzas?" Joseph asked.

"Lunar control is in Brigit Markz in ship 461. We are launching. We have five souls on board."

"Hi Brigit, you into pizza delivery now?"

"You saw that?"

"Yup, sure did. Cameras everywhere, you know."

"Understood control. We will intercept my car, making a slow but leisurely beeline for Mars."

"MARS?" Joseph said.

"Understood, Brigit. You are clear to leave Lunar space and head to Mars at whatever speed you choose."

"Thanks, Mark. Have a good day."

"Safe flight."

They disconnected.

Joseph said, "We're headed to Mars?"

Virginia replied, "Of course we are. We have pizza to deliver."

Joseph said quietly, "Pizza to deliver, of course. What was I thinking?"

Brigit asked the Lieutenant, "Can you fly in a straight line?" He started laughing, "OK, here's their transponder bleep. Head to it at a comfortable speed."

"He programmed the screen to give directional headings until it found its mark a minute later. "Got them. Heading at 80% power. Be there in 90 minutes."

Magda asked, "How soon till they hit Mars?"

Tommy pressed a few buttons. "About two hours from now. We will catch up to them when they enter Mars space."

Magda said, "Ship, call car 324."

Rory answered, "Hi, Boss!"

From out of sight, "How's my car?" Brigit asked.

"V was right to put us in here. The sensor pack requires us to constantly adjust and readjust our heading as it randomly fires and throws us off course."

"But…." Brigit questioned from off camera.

"The car is fine. It may need vacuuming, though; Rory eats a breakfast biscuit, which crumbles easily like she hangs out on a farm or something!" Mik said. The camera flipped to him as he spoke. Brigit started laughing.

Magda took over the conversation, "Guys, we are 90 minutes from you. We have Pizza. You are likely to be dirtside in two hours."

"Which puts us landing at 1600, perfect!" Mik answered. Magda winked, and the call disconnected.

The sensor pack was transmitted at an encrypted frequency to the shuttle and directly to Virginia's console. She was getting spikes of some type of odd radiation.

"I think I found something?" She said, not quite sure what she was actually seeing.

Joseph and Magda stood behind her, "I have seen this before," Joseph said. Looking at the radiation levels, "Let's see if I am interpreting this right. The background base level is .3 sievert and there, and there is a spike of 4 sievert. That's bad, but the EM shield on the car protects Rory and Mik."

Virginia jumped in, "Kinda bad is an understatement. In an unprotected craft, bad things can happen. Brigit, in your report, I read about the worm analysis. They were essentially slightly radioactive but nothing specific or hazardous to humans. They are successeptible to salt, so mixing salt in the dirt will neutralize the radiation and kill the worms."

"Not just any salt. It must be diethylenetriamine pentaacetate. Mixed in the soil, it will bind with the radioactive elements of the worms and neutralize them. Some will die, but let's call that organic fertilizer."

Magda said, "I have not heard mention of DTPA in decades. Let me see if I can find some, and we can run a test on a single field."

Magda went off to a far corner and made a few calls. About an hour later, she joined the group again.

"OK, the Navy has a DTPA stockpile on a ship near Mars. They are heading there now."

Brigit asked, "How much do they have with them?"

"Apparently, enough to treat the entire surface of Mars. I told the good Admiral we only need a few pounds to validate our hypothesis."

Brigit added, "For the field, I am thinking about cleaning up first, maybe a pound and a half. For all of colonized Mars, maybe ten pounds. If memory serves me right, the organic life must be evacuated for a few days, and the entire dome will be treated. It can be blown in through life-support and propagate on the airwaves. Once it is all imparted, the ventilation can be turned off for a day. Once it is all settled, reinhabiting the dome should be OK. Worst case, headache and nausea from 5% of the population." Brigit froze. She was looking directly at Tommy.

"General, she's doing that voodoo thing again," Tommy said.

No one spoke, and she snapped out of it.

"OK, what did you see?" Virginia asked.

"Tommy, your sister is very sensitive to the DTPA and will get sick. She will feel better in a couple weeks but will need constant assistance. A nurse is under her dome, the first dome we are testing on. However, the nurse will be required to work in other places. Still, 7% of the population will have adverse side effects, and the only three nurses will be stretched thin." She paused, "This does fix the crops. Putting an EM shield on the dirt haulers will keep it from reoccurring."

"What if I tell you that the Navy ship heading for Mars is a medical ship," Magda added, "Suppose they are directed to stay and render aid by providing medical aid to the population."

Brigit smiled at her boss, "That would do it."

"Ship," Magda said, "Priority call to the skipper of the Nightengale."

The ship's captain appeared, and Magda spoke, "Doctor Captain Bragg! You are placed under my purview for about a month. Remain in Mars orbit, and I will fill you in personally."

"Understood, General. Nice to see you again, by the way."

Magda turned to the others on her ship, "Bertha here was my doctor for a year when she was but a young pup, a mere Captain, I mean Lieutenant. You are still Navy, right?

"Yes, dear, I am." Those on her bridge laughed, "By the way, I took a page from the leadership book of Rochavarro, and I tend to treat those under me as friends. They know when playful Bertha, serious Bertha, or upset Bertha is talking to them."

Magda addressed the bridge, "OK, Bridge crew. Is that true?"

In one voice, there was a YES GENERAL.

"I look forward to seeing all of you tomorrow. You and your key people should meet me at the club at 2100 tonight. The first round is on me. I hope you like scotch?" Magda said.

"As long as it is good stuff!" Came from off-camera.

"OK, who said that?"

Bertha laughed, "My XO, the former Commander Mills."

Magda laughed, "OK, then. I got his bar tab all night."

They talked for a few more minutes and disconnected.

Magda looked at Virginia, "Call the car, fill them in. Then, call Mars, Tommy's sister, and have her meet us at the terminal. She must be on board with all this and know the possibilities without the exact circumstances. Tommy boy, you will be temporarily assigned to the medical corp to aid your sister!"

Tommy smiled at his boss. She is, by far, the most excellent boss in the universe.

~~~~~~~~~~~

The conversation with Teressa Reilley went well. Teressa thought the benefits outweighed the danger. No one told her she would get the sickest, but Tommy informed her he would be assigned to Mars for a month to watch over the reclamation project. They are calling that so the universe will not know the real issues. The first week was to impregnate the soil with ultra-fine powder, the next two weeks were to play caregiver, and the last was a vacation.

The pair of spacecraft approached Mars, and they needed to retract the sensor pack and stow it for landing.

Rory called on the comm, "Virginia, the winch is jammed. It will not retract."

Virginia trained the scanner on the pack, followed it down the cable to the trunk, and saw a small rock jammed in the cable intake.

"Well, got good news and bad news. The good news is it's easy to fix. The bad news is one of us will nccd to fix it. There a rock jammed where the cable enters the winch."

"I'll do it!" Joseph volunteered, "I love a good space walk. Besides, that means I get to play with the jets."

Magda said, "You sure about that?"

Joseph replied, "I am."

Everyone looked at Brigit, "Well, no vision. Have fun."

Everyone on the ship donned their full space suit, and they drained the ship of air. Joseph grabbed a sturdy, flat-blade screwdriver and attached it to his belt. Then, he held the small jet system and jumped toward his wife's car about a hundred feet away.

Joseph hit the car and grabbed onto the winch. He looked at the rock, "Uh, guys. This is worse than we thought. The winch is fried. Basically junk at this point."

"OK, now what?" Tommy asked.

"I got an idea," Joseph said. "Let me cut the cable and bring it all into the shuttle. Then we can both land without a concern."

Virginia added, "Stow it into the cargo door outside the ship. In case it is retaining anything bad for people."

"Understood. I need to grab a pair of cutters."

"I'll bring them to you," Magda said, "Besides, I like zero-G as much as you do."

Magda prepped, jumped like Joseph, and landed softly beside his left arm. "Damn! If we were closer, I would suggest removing it and tossing it into the sun! Here are the cutters."

Joseph grabbed them and cut the cable at the winch. It was very slow going and took a minute. She reached her left arm, shut off her transmitter, and then touched the transmitter off toggle on Joseph's sleeve. He looked at her a moment, and they tapped helmets.

A few seconds later, they restarted their transmitters. Magda moved to Joseph's right side, holding the cable so they did not have to chase it. As soon as it cut through, the retro rockets on the pack fired for a second, pulling Magda off the car. Joseph grabbed her and pulled her back.

"Well, that was fun!" Magda said. "OK. We're heading back to the shuttle. You two stop lolly-gagging and head to where you need to be."

They both said, "Yes, Boss," simultaneously. And headed to Mars.

Magda and Joseph stowed the pack in the hold, tied it down, and returned to the ship. Closing the door, the air returned, and they removed their helmets.

"OK. Bring us in and park us."

They entered the thin Mars atmosphere and headed to the bay as the doors opened. Brigit entered the large bay, and Biff said where to park. She hovered, taxied, and parked perfectly. Exiting the shuttle, they saw the grav cart, loaded it with five boxes, and headed for the bay offices.

As they arrived at the bay office, Magda yelled as the group entered, **"Did someone order pizza?"**

The room was so floored by the statement no one called the room to attention. Biff spoke.

"AH! Finally. My pizza delivery is here," he said, looking at the General. "Excuse me, are you a new delivery person?"

"It's a part-time thing. I do it once a decade," She said to him, "We're square now, right?"

"Yes, Ma'am. We're square!" Everyone just looked at him, staring blankly. The General owed him a favor?

"You know, you could have asked for any favor in the universe but asked for a pizza delivery for these people. Look at them, staring blindly, mouths hanging open. Was it worth it?"

Biff replied, "Well, these are Mars's most animate, intelligent people under normal circumstances. I guess seeing a General deliver pizzas to me blew their poor little minds."

Magda yelled, "Where are those herbivores?" Four hands went up, "This is your box. The rest of you," She looked at Biff, "How many diners do you have?"

"19."

"Well, you got 20 pizzas. So, share and have a good little party. There should be a lot of leftovers, so take home everything or share with friends," She looked at Biff, "May I suggest you call the Colonel to an impromptu, important, and urgent meeting?"

Biff grinned, "Room, please notify the Colonel. His presence is urgently requested in the landing bay office." The computer beeped.

"I may just wait till he gets here to see his face."

A minute later, "Biff, you called? Wait, General, to what do I owe this honor?"

"Just making a pizza delivery. Have fun with the crew. They are my favorite crew on any planet."

"Oh, General. This came for you this morning," he said. He handed her an envelope.

She opened it and looked it over. Shaking her head. "Virginia, come here and sign this, please." She did and smiled when she saw what it was, "Lieutenant Colonel Spencer, you're next," He signed it and smiled as well.

The General looked around, "OK, who's going to award this?" No one said a word.

Finally, Joseph spoke, "I'll do it."

He walked to Magda and looked at the certificate. Magda had spoken to him when they were outside, comms off and bumping helmets. A genuinely private communication.

Joseph spoke, "Brigit Markz, please come here." She approached him, "It is my greatest pleasure to award you your full pilot's license for all known craft within reason." He handed her the certificate and the card she would present before a flight if she was not a known pilot.

The room applauded and cheered.

Joseph hugged and kissed his wife, and the rest of the room hugged or shook her hand. She had been with this group a lot over the years and knew most of them and their families.

Magda and her gang left the room, leaving the party to go for itself. As she was walking out the door, "Oh, gang. Hit the club when your next shift ends. I'll let the bartender know you get one drink on me! " She looked at the colonel.

"Me too!" The Colonel said.

"Sure, why not." The room applauded.

Mik added, "I think the Macallan Scotch is an amazing taste sensation."

From somewhere down the hall, Magda yelled, "MIK SPENCER, you're a dead man!" He winked at the group and left.

He caught up to his group, "No worries, Boss, I'll split the bar bill with ya."

~~~~~~~~~~~~

"Who's hungry?" Brigit asked.

All hands went up.

"The Club?" Magda asked.

"Dining hall!" Brigit said.

They all looked at her and then slowly started nodding.

"Burger, fries, soft drink." She said, "Wait. Onion rings!"

The group stopped, turned left, and headed to the dining hall. Magda added, "The Club after dinner!"

~~~~~~~~~~~~

As they entered the Chow Hall, they were talking about their meals. Burgers, fried chicken, pot pie, meatloaf, spaghetti, and meatballs. Of course, Joseph and Mik chose the SOS. The others looked at them and said, "Really!"

Joseph jumped up, "Forgot?"

He returned with a bowl of English peas heated till a little soft in butter.

"Peas?" Brigit asked as Joseph and Mik spooned them over their SOS. "I suppose that makes it all better?"

"Not just better," Mik said.

"More better!" Joseph finished.

They clicked spoons and dug in.

Brigit reached over and took a small fork of Joseph's meal. "Not nearly as bad as I thought."

"OK, we need a game plan!" Magda said as Teressa walked up.

"Found you!" She smiled, "Club or here. After a flight from Earth, these are the two most likely places you will be."

Tommy said to his sister after a good hug, "You hungry?"

"Nope. Had dinner a few minutes ago. Pork roast, mashed potatoes, peas. It was excellent! Coffee sounds good."

Tommy said, "Sit. I'll get it for you." He walked away, and she sat in his seat. A minute later, he returned and handed her a cup of coffee with cream. She took a sip.

"PERFECT! You remember."

"Yup, two sugars and two cream squirts." He pulled up another chair to sit between Teressa and Magda. They both scooted over a bit to give him room. "Anyone in need of a refill before I sit?"

Everyone held their cup in the air. He started laughing and walked to another table with a serving tray. He put the cups on the tray and hit the coffee urn again. A few minutes later, he returned.

"This thing gets heavy when they are all full," He doled out the cups.

Brigit asked, curious, "How do you know the cups are right for the right person?"

"Simple. I put them on the tray starting at this mark, in rank order or alphabetically for the chiefs and you and Joseph."

His sister nearly spit her coffee and started laughing at that statement. "You people really are all friends and a little nuts!"

Magda replied, "Thanks for noticing."

Everyone saw her face change, and the tone of the conversation went to the project. "Teressa, you got worms, and we can fix it in a few days, a week more than likely. Several, more like 10 percent, may get sick, but not hospital sick. Maybe thinking they need a hospital, but it will pass in a few days, and full recuperation after another week."

She looked at the people around the table, "OK, what's the plan?"

Brigit outlined the plan, her dome first. They talked about the chemicals, the worms, and the corn, and how they determined what caused it and how to avoid it from happening again. Every living creature must be evacuated, so they must be evacuated one dome at a time. They need a place to house the displaced dome inhabitants, the livestock, and the pets.

As a group, they all stood and headed to their homes. Or rooms, or wherever. The plan was to get the room squared away, then stop into the club for a drink.

Tommy went home with his sister. Magda entered the VOQ with an entourage, and their rooms were ready. Magda is in one room, Mik is in another, the Chiefs are in another, and Brigit and Joseph are in another.

Magda said, "Whose room is first?"

"Mine," Mik said. He opened the door; lights were on, soft music played, and candles were lit. "Hello?" He said.

"Come in and close the door." He recognized the voice; it was his wife.

"See you at breakfast, Monica," Brigit said.

"Possibly…." Monica said, and Mik closed the door.

The rest of the group organized their rooms for a few minutes, and it was near the time to meet the Navy in the club.

Magda walked in and motioned to the club manager, who understood. "Yes, General, how can I assist you?"

"Have you a secluded room I can use for a couple of hours for a private meeting?"

"I do, General. It is down that hall and seats 15 comfortably. 20 if you are friendly."

"I need it this evening if it is available."

"Follow me," and the club manager walked down the hall.

They entered the room, which was set up like a private bar. Magda walked to the bar and looked. She had a disappointed look on her face.

"Where's the good scotch?"

He spoke into his sleeve, and a minute later, a case of Macallan, an 18-year-old scotch, appeared in the room. Magda smiled, "All we need is ice."

As she said it, a large ice bucket walked into the room, carried by a tall, robust young man.

"Perfect!" Magda said, "There will be a few Navy people showing up. Direct them back here, please."

Magda's team poured themselves a drink and sat on one side of the table. A few minutes later, the Navy appeared.

Virginia said, as they entered the room, "Pour yourselves a drink and have a seat. We all need to talk." She paused, "Does anyone need food?"

No one needed food. They all grabbed a drink and sat.

Magda opened the meeting by introducing Warrant Officer 3 Rory Mitchell and Virginia Rolf. She mentioned her XO, Lieutenant Colonel Mik Spencer, was unavailable, which made Rory and Virginia grin slightly.

"So, you are the XO, commander."

"Yes, Ma'am."

"You speak your mind?"

"Yes, Ma'am."

She stood and put a bottle of the excellent scotch in front of him, "Will that do?"

"Definitely, General. You have good taste, may I add."

The meeting lasted a couple of hours. The result was that the ship was put at General Rochavarro's convenience.

They talked for over an hour and knew what needed to be done.

~~~~~~~~~~~

"Room. Send a message to the Club manager. I will be there later today to settle the dome teams bar tab." It was signed by General M. Rochavarro.

She finished getting dressed, and a message came in: THANKS GENERAL.

The vid rang, "Answer!"

"Magda, how are you this morning?"

"Hungry mostly and in need of coffee. What's up, Boss?"

"It got approved. As of five minutes ago. I'll send the orders to the secure printer in the Colonel's office."

"Thanks, boss. This is going to be fun." They disconnected, "Room, call room 8."

Monica answered, "Where's that man of yours?"

"Right here, boss, what's up?"

"Just notified, the orders came in. Printing in the Colonel's office as we speak."

Mik got a grin, "Sweet! They have no clue."

"Nope. Took me half a year, but it's done."

Mik asked, "Where?"

"Where this all started."

"The bay."

"Yup, the bay. You call Biff. I'll call the Colonel."

They disconnected.

Mik said, "Room, call Master Sergeant Wellington."

"Hi, Colonel. What's up?"

"We will be there after breakfast to check how the party went last night, but that is not why we are coming to the bay."

"It ain't?"

"Nope. The promotion orders for the Chiefs finally came through. It took the general half a year to push it through the red tape, but it's done. The orders are being printed on the Colonel's printer, and he will also be in the bay office. How would you like to take an active role in the promotion?"

"I would be honored. What can I do?"

"Head to the quartermaster and get a few CAPTAIN rank tabs, and when you get the nod, remove WO3 and replace it with CAPT."

"I love it. Consider it done!" The call disconnected, and Mik and his wife walked into the hall as the others left their rooms.

"Damn, I love breakfast!" Joseph said, "My favorite morning meal. I think the biscuit and gravy was better today than normal."

Magda said, "Let's go to the bay and see how it all went yesterday. I hope the pizza was a hit."

The group walked about five minutes to the bay offices and entered the room where someone, the Colonel, called the room to attention at the arrival of the General.

Magda looked at him, "If you do that again, Biff will outrank you!" They hugged briefly.

Magnus looked at the group. They were all in casual uniforms, meaning their rank and name tabs were also on the uniform. "Got this on the printer this morning – it's for you. I may start charging you a print fee."

"If you do, no more pizza!" Biff laughed, as did a few others in the room.

"Who's gonna tell them about this?" Magnus asked.

"You do it. I wanna watch." General MagdaLynne Rochavarro said to her friend.

"OK." He removed the papers from the sleeve. In a very military voice, "ATTENTION TO ORDERS." The entire room came to attention,

"This is to recognize the accomplishments and the abilities of two well-known individuals in this room. Chief Rory Mitchell and Chief Virginia Rolf. You are at this moment promoted to the permanent rank of Captain." He paused and saluted the two former chiefs, "God help us all!"

Mik walked up front, "As a Captain, you need to retake the oath."

Rory and Virginia were floored.

The oath was recited, and Mik saluted the new captains. Then hugged them both. Monica and Brigit gave them both a congratulatory hug.

"BIFF! You're up!" Mik said.

Biff approached them and replaced the WO3 with a CAPT rank on their uniform. As he did each rank tab, he saluted the new Captain. The room exploded. Tommy started laughing at the thought.

"What's so funny?" The Colonel asked.

"Well, sir, it just hit me: those two outrank me again." Tommy laughed, as did several others. "But, on this team, rank ain't no big thing. Everyone does what they do, and the machine is oiled and runs smoothly."

"Damn boy, that is philosophical?"

"Thank you, Colonel. My degree is in philosophy and religion."

"And I see you have your work cut out for you. Do the horns ever pop out?" He was referring to Magda, who had that look on her face.

"No sir, never! At least not in public," He fake whispered.

Magda cleared her throat. They looked at her and both said, "Crap!"

They all quieted down a bit. Magda said to the bay workers, "You people are horrible! Who in their right mind told you about the most amazing scotch in the universe?"

Everyone pointed at Mik, who raised his hand.

"I seem to have an opening for a Lieutenant Colonel on my staff. Anyone want to apply?" Magda said, joking.

The room roared when Biff raised his hand.

CHAPTER NINE

"Mars control, this is car 324," Virginia said.

The entire group spent the month on Mars, ensuring the worm crisis was averted and the corn crops returned to nominal.

"Car 324, you leaving us?"

"That we are, heading home finally."

"I take it the shuttle will be departing soon also?"

Brigit's voice could be heard, "That is correct, control. Shuttle 461 is finishing up preflight, and we're leaving also."

"You know," The controller said, "That little car will fit in the bay of that great big shuttle."

"We know. The plan is to hit Mars orbit, then slip into the bay and fly home with us faster than that little car can get them there."

"Good plan. So, Car 324, you are cleared to hit space. As for Shuttle 461, you ready?"

"Car 324, launching," Virginia said.

"We are," Tommy replied to the controller.

"Brigit, your voice changed." They laughed a little, "OK, Shuttle 461, you are cleared to hit space as well. Nothing in or outbound for 25 minutes, so the orbit and parking in the bay are cleared and approved."

"Thanks. Shuttle 461 launching."

As they made orbit, the shuttle found the car and pulled up next to them, then in front slightly. Virginia parked and secured the vehicle in the bay after the space doors closed. She went into the passenger area.

"All set." She grabbed a seat, and Brigit and Tommy set course for Earth, or more precisely, the Moon, to drop off the hot boxes.

"Brigit dear, we seem to still be accelerating," Magda said.

"Quite perceptive, Magda. I have never flown this thing at 100% power and wanted to see how it felt."

Rory said, "If you keep that up for 25 minutes, we'll be home."

"Ship, call the farm," Joseph said.

Jonathan appeared on the screen, "Heading home finally?"

"Yup!"

"Good. Magda there?"

"I am."

"Gayle and I went to the station, grabbed Fuzzy, and brought her to our house. She and Serena have been best buds for more than three weeks now," He shook his head, "...and for some reason, they both love to use me as a bed."

"How did you get into my cabin?" Magda asked.

"You're kidding, right? You know that everyone in the solar system knows your entry code and that most of the station plays with your baby when you are away."

"I suspected," She smiled.

"Well, when you bring back our wayward neighbors, you can pick up Fuzzy."

"Sounds like a solid plan."

Gayle took over the conversation, "I heard from Marissa. She took the comm from the cave and brought it home with her. Glad she did, too. It seems there was a small drone flying over the community before dawn yesterday. I guess it was a sightseeing tour of the mountain. She was the only one awake, milking volunteer, so no one else noticed it. It was silent, she said, but it hovered over her a moment, and she got a good look at it, and I suppose it got a good look at her, too!"

"So, has the timeline for us meeting the elders moved up?" Brigit asked.

"No," Jon replied, "But Mark, Ramona, and Lil' Bit all shared a dream. One week from tomorrow, the invasion starts at the cave."

"OK, then we will prepare to meet them at the cave," Magda said. She turned to Rory, "You still meeting the Commander at the farm?"

Rory replied, "I am. We talked a few days ago. He told me about the community he found and reported it to his bosses. Then, he asked me how long I had known about it. I asked him what made him think I knew, and he said my face had no amazement or curiosity. I took a page from Brigit and told the truth."

Brigit smiled, "Well, at the farm, we will all 'come clean,' I believe that is the right phrase. It sounds as though he will be on our side in this," she paused momentarily. "Rory, is this man about your height? He has dark brown wavy hair and blue eyes."

"He is. How did you know?" She paused a heartbeat, "AH! A vision about him. So, I take it it's all good then?"

"Yes, is it," Brigit smiled, as did Joseph. She told her husband that he and Rory would be married in less than a year. They would have a long and very joyous relationship. But, of course, she could not say anything to Rory.

"Chief... I mean Captain Rolf. Still ain't got used to that, but I need for you to set up shelters for 20 people out of the way," She turned to Rory, "Get everyone there BEFORE they all show up," She turned to Jon, "Get with Marissa and tell her to meet us at the cave in three days. What's the weather forecast for the next week?"

Virginia tapped a few points on her pad, "At the settlement, temps will be below zero at night and maybe 32°F for a daytime high. Possible snow flurries are forecasted to occur in a few days. So, I guess the first snow thing is gonna happen."

Magda said, "OK, we'll be home and at the farm in less than an hour. Since the Commander is expected this evening, Rory will remain at Brigit and Joseph's house. The rest of us will set up the cave for a pow-wow. I need to make a few calls, too."

Brigit looked at Rory, "One room or two?" She had a grin on her face that said it all.

"Let's play it by ear," Rory replied.

Magda laughed, "Ship, call Pie in the Sky Pizza in the lunar colony."

"Howdy, General. On your way home, finally?"

"We are. Got 5 hot boxes filled with cookies. We are on a tight schedule, and if you can meet us at the port, I would be thrilled."

"For those cookies, I would walk to Mars. When you are on final, give me a jingle. Wait, are all five hot boxes filled with cookies?"

"Yes, sorry. We had so much time on our hands I just kept buying you cookies. Is 144 too many?"

"General, I owe you dinner next time you are in town."

~~~~~~~~~~

The car landed on the apron and emptied. Magda, Brigit, Joseph, Rory, Tommy, Teressa, Mik, Virginia, and Monica exited and headed into Brigit's house.

"Looks like a clown car!" Jon said, "People just keep getting out," Jon looked at Brigit, "So, kid. Where's your car? I know you left with it."

Magda replied, "Perfect then, we are at the three-ring circus!"

"My car is at the station; someone wants to look over the structure and remove a dead winch before they give it back to me."

Jon winked at Virginia.

Rory went to her room at Brigit and Joseph's farm and changed. The others all found their rooms and changed also. Placing all of the pressure suits in the car, Tommy and his sister would take them back to the station and get them prepped for next use.

"Teressa prefers the station over the Earth. She said no dome makes her nervous." Tommy said to the group. "Besides, you people are nuts!"

Everyone made strange noises, and Tommy shook his head. Teressa started laughing.

~~~~~~~~~

Mik and Monica did what they do best, cook. But, this time, they made sandwiches, and everyone ended up at Gayle and Jon's, so that's where the food was!

Magda walked in and sat in a comfy chair. Fuzzy hopped up on her and gave her a hug, then Serena hopped up and did the same. They curled up and fell asleep in her lap.

Mik said, "Hey, Boss. Since you are currently being used as a bed, do you want us to make you a sandwich?"

"Thanks, Mik, whatcha got?"

"Roast beef, turkey, chicken salad, chips...."

"Roast beef with something like Swiss cheese, plain chips, cold glass of tea."

They made her sandwich, and Monica delivered it. She put the glass on the side table and handed her the plate. "You do like horseradish sauce?"

"I do, why?"

"We found some in the fridge and spread it on the bread. Pretty good, I might say."

She took a bite of the meal and said, "Damn, that is good!"

The rest all made or grabbed an already-created sandwich. Mik made his and put a bunch of potato chips on it, and the others all stared. As he took a bite, it crunched. The rest of the group opened their sandwich, put a few chips on theirs, and happily took a considerable bite.

Rory walked in, but she had a guest with her.

"Hi, gang. Let me introduce my friend, Commander Marcel Romet."

He saw the general on the chair and looked shocked to see that there was a general in the group. Magda saw the look on his face and spoke, "Marcel, first off, I am not just a general; I am also a human and a female. So, when I am not in uniform, I am off the clock."

Rory looked at him and said, "We all just call her Boss."

He looked around, "Uh, OK. Thanks, Boss!"

"See, now that didn't hurt," Magda said.

Mik asked, "You hungry?"

"I am. Came straight here from my station and didn't have a chance to grab anything."

Brigit said, "Station 4, right." He looked shocked; that station was a secure location. "By the way, when you return to your desk, the paper you are looking for fell off the back of your desk. It is lodged between the wall and the back right leg."

"Great, tha…." He started to say, then changed the sentence, "Wait, you have been to my office? When? I do not remember any visitors ever."

"Nope, never been there. But a friend told me about it, and I thought I would let you know so you don't miss the chance to go on that trip. I think you call it TAD?"

"Yes, TAD, Temporary Attached Duty. But who, how?"

Magda said, "Marcel. The next things you hear are classified. Suppose you have any questions about their accuracy or reality. In that case, you must contact Admiral Russell and simply say, THE COMMUNITY. He will understand and secure the line; you can ask any question, and he will answer honestly. He knows you are here, and we are having this conversation."

"What did you get me into, Lion?" He called her by a pet name; she looked embarrassed, and he realized what he did, "Forget I said that…."

"OH NO, " Virginia said, "I need more info."

Rory sighed and said, "Well, Rory…. Ror…. ROAR…. Lion!"

"COOL!" Virginia said, "You are now my favorite kitty."

"Oh, dear lord," Rory said, and everyone laughed.

Brigit said, "Grab some food and a drink and have a seat. We need to talk."

Everyone outlined the entire community, and Brigit, Joseph, Gayle, and Jon were born and grew up there. Roughly an hour and a half later, they all finished talking. Virginia turned off the monitor, which displayed a real-time community scan.

Magda said, "I know you have questions, Marcel. So, ask away. We will be honest and as detailed as possible."

After another hour, he felt like he had a data hose shoved in his mouth, filled with new and unfamiliar information.

Marcel said, "I am sorry, but I passed it on to my boss already."

"We know. We also know the team will appear at the cave and cliff a few hours from the settlement in a week. We plan to be there a few days before and set up a hotel. The elders from the community will meet us there, and the leadership can discuss the next steps."

"Wait. How do you know when they will be there, and for that matter, who?" Marcel asked.

Magda said, "May as well tell him, kid."

Brigit said, "My first husband was there in the room when you made the discovery, and he told me. He also told me about the excursion the Captains above you planned and who will be on the team."

"Your first husband?"

"He died five years ago. As a wandering spirit, he sees things. He stopped in and let me know."

"Wait. A ghost?"

"He prefers to be called a wandering spirit. He really dislikes ghosts. It is so negative," Joseph said.

Gayle got a strange look on her face. Brigit smiled, "Hi, Brad."

"He's here?" Magda said.

"He is. Standing next to Rory, actually." Brigit laughed, then nodded, "He commented that you two are made for each other. I agree."

"How do I know you are on the level?" Marcel asked.

Virginia said, "Give him the Rory test."

"OK." She went to the bookcase and asked Marcel, "Pick a book?"

"The yellow one on the far left," Marcel said.

Brigit started laughing.

"What's so funny?" Rory asked.

"Brad hates poetry."

Virginia handed him the book, "Here you go."

Rory said, "Now, open to any random page and pick a few lines. Brad will read them to Brigit, and she will repeat them."

He pointed to a stanza on a page. Brigit cracked up.

She composed herself and said, "I find it interesting that you chose that poem, Friendly Ghosts. I remember seeing this poem when I stayed here for the first time nearly five years ago. OK, Brad. Read away."

She recited the poem as Brad said the words. He flipped a few pages and pointed; she followed suit, and he did it a few other times. Then, at the front of the book, he pointed to the Library of Earth information, and Brigit recited it.

"OK, I believe you now. But…."

Brigit cut him off, "Brad is moving on. He stayed until he knew we would be OK, and now he can continue his journey," A moment later, "He's gone. Maybe for the last time."

They talked till midnight about the community, Brigit and Joseph, Brad, Serena, Gayle and Jonathon, and everything. Marcel became the newest member of this happy little group.

~~~~~~~~~~~

Marcel found himself alone with the General in the barn. The prep was all completed. They were heading to the cave. He liked this group. A lot. They are honest, true, loyal, and genuine friends. Granted, they all know their place, but that is a sign of a great leader, or in this case, leaders. Magda and Mik lead by example. They go, and the others follow.

"General, I have a question for you?" Marcel said.

"I know you do, and the answer is yes."

"But I have not asked the question?"

"Brigit saw this moment a few days ago, and the question you were about to ask is, can you become a member of my team, right?"

Marcel looked amazed, "It is."

"If you call into the office, you will discover orders waiting for you that reassign you to me," she grinned. "I also know that you will ask Rory to be your mate, and she will say yes. You will be married on the station and honeymoon in a few places the two of you always wanted to go on Earth, and finally, your extended honeymoon will end on the Moon with an extended reception, a second reception, almost as large as the first. You cannot tell her about this until the Moon reception or after it."

Marcel looked shocked.

"Now, don't look at me like that. Tell me you have not thought of Rory in that way?"

"Well, I have. I planned this a few weeks ago, and her invite gave me the idea she would say yes when or if I asked," He pulled a ring out of his pocket, "I will be giving this to her before we head out. I am worried as to her answer."

"Do what I do. Talk to Brigit for a moment."

"Talk to me for what?" Brigit said as she walked into the barn. Magda patted him on the shoulder and walked out. Winking to Brigit as she left.

"The Boss suggested I show this to you."

He opened the ring box, and Brigit saw the ring for the first time. She froze.

A few seconds later, she started up again.

"OK, I take it you needed me to see what would happen if you asked Rory in the next hour. I saw it. She will be here in a few minutes to grab the car. You got down on one knee and showed her the ring, and she started crying, took you, and kissed you. You placed the ring on her finger, and in six months, you are married. You have a very long and very happy life together."

Marcel was shocked, amazed, and relieved all at the same time.

"One last thing. Don't mention this little talk. It was for you, not her," She turned and started walking out the door. As she left the barn, "Hi, Rory. You here to grab the car?"

"I am; I figure it would be an asset to our little group at the cave. Smaller and faster."

"Good thought. Go for it."

Brigit went to the house, and Rory entered the barn.

"Marcel, what are you…." She said as she walked into the barn.

"I figured you would be in here, and I hoped to catch you alone," he said. She noticed he looked nervous.

"Look, what's wrong. You look like you have a lit explosive in your pants."

Without saying anything, he slowly lowered himself onto one knee and held the open ring box to her. She began to cry. He put the ring on her finger, and they hugged, kissed, and held each other.

"So, I take it the answer is yes."

All she could do was nod and squeak out a YES.

A few minutes later, they went to the house. They walked in together, and no one said anything. It took a minute, but Virginia saw the ring and exploded.

Everyone was happy for the two of them.

~~~~~~~~~~~

Once they arrived at the cave, they all grabbed rooms. They knew the group from the community would be there for dinner, and the group investigating would come in the morning.

"Gayle, this is Marissa." Came over to her portable comm.

"Hi, Marissa. We are here at the cave, all setup and waiting for you. Are you warm enough?"

"Yes, we are all fine. Ramona, Marshall, Mark, Serena, and Louise, We should be there in a few hours."

"Marissa, this is Virginia. We have you and estimate an hour and forty-five minutes at your current speed."

"Even better, chief."

"Marissa, I got the promotions for them through," Magda said.

"Well then, congratulations to the new Captains."

Rory asked, "How long have you been working on that?"

Magda grinned, "Quite a while. Call if you need us. We can be to you in minutes."

"Understood. Cart out."

Maybe an hour later, Virginia sent up a flare, "Boss, there is an issue. They seem to be stuck or really slow, and where they are is being hit by a blizzard. Temps are taking a nosedive, too. Can I grab the car and bring most of them back here?"

"Do it. Also, grab two sets of winter survival gear. Bring back all but two volunteers, but give them the gear to wear. Put thermal blankets on the horses."

"Understood."

Rory helped her load the car, and Virginia launched. She made it to them in ten minutes.

She landed the car in the blizzard and popped a flare. The cart made its way to her, and she put the blankets on the horses first, then pulled out the winter gear and handed it to Mark and Marshall.

"Put this on," She said. A few minutes later, they were dressed in the gear.

"Wow! This is nice," Mark said.

Marshall said, "I take it we bring the cart the rest of the way, and you fly everyone else in the car?"

"You are good!" She handed him a comm, "See you in about an hour. Call if you need anything," and returned to the car.

A minute later, she launched, and the cart made its way to the cave.

Virginia landed at the cave, and Serena jumped out of the car and ran straight to Brigit, "Aunt Brigit. I'm Serena. Grama told me all about you before she left."

Magda said, "So she…." Brigit nodded to Magda, "Weird, but also cool."

She grabbed Magda and hugged her, "I remember you from my picture. Grama said you are the greatest, and when I see you, I need to give you a big hug for her since she can't give it to you herself."

Magda asked, "How old are you, Serena?"

"I am almost 6 now," Her face twisted. They all knew the look. She unfroze and looked at her Mom. "Mommy, the men from the other place will be here before breakfast. They will be hungry, and I know what they want for breakfast. If we cook them breakfast, they will be friendly, right?"

"Yes, they will, kiddo," Magda said, "So, tell Rory and Marcel what they need for breakfast, and if you want something special, tell them also."

Serena told Rory and Marcel the favorite breakfast for each of the four investigators and that she liked panacakes. They hopped into the car and headed off. Magda grabbed the comm.

"Car 324, bring back a nice dinner from the station, which is where I take it you are headed."

Marcel replied, "Correct, Boss. We'll find something tasty for the gang."

CHAPTER
TEN

The car returned, and everyone unloaded it into the galley module. Mik was in his element. He loves to cook, as does Ramona. He started putting the breakfast items away, and Ramona came in to help. She put the hot trays in the warmer and the cold trays in the cooler.

Ramona asked, "So, what did you get for dinner?" It was just the two of them in the kitchen. Everyone else was in the main building, a few feet away, but you needed to go outside to get there.

"Build your own tacos. We have the meat, or rather the meats and all the veggies you can dream up. Hard and soft, or flour or corn tortillas as well. We brought back water and fruit juice as

181

an additive for the adults. We'll eat when the cart arrives, and the horses are secured, fed, and watered in the warm building of theirs."

"I had tacos for the first time on the last trip, and I love them."

They put everything away and prepared things for breakfast. There will be 15 for breakfast, so presetting things will make life easier in the morning.

A car landed, and someone exited. It launched again. Monica walked into the kitchen.

"I see. I spend time at work, and you find a new sous chef?" She joked.

Mik turned at the voice and ran to her; Ramona said, "He means nothing to me other than dinner, breakfast, and maybe lunch."

"I know what you mean. But, to me, he has other uses…." The women laughed.

Mik said, "I feel like a side of beef suddenly." He smiled. "But I'm okay with that!"

Ramona and Monica hugged, and together, the three of them got dinner ready.

The cart arrived an hour later, but the horses and the humans were all comfortable in their winter attire.

They had a small 'barn' set up for the horses, basically a large room, but it had heat, food, and water for them. Mark and Marshall went to the big room and removed the winter gear after getting the horses squared away with Joseph.

"I like those clothes. I could have stayed out in that blizzard for days." Marshall said.

Mark added, "However, I am delighted to be in this toasty little building."

~~~~~~~~~~

Mik walked to a wall panel and hit the big green button.

"Everyone, come over to the galley building. Dinner is ready."

He released the button, walked back to the counter, and waited. The first one in was Serena, holding Magda's hand. The others followed. Mik quieted everyone down once they were all in and the door was closed.

"OK." Marcel said, "We thought about it, and the Captain here decided what we are serving you all for dinner. So if you don't like it, you know who to talk to!" He smiled.

Rory said, "I figured with this group, the easiest thing to make and serve is to serve yourself. So, I made a few calls as we approached the station, and Marcel and I picked up a make-your-own taco bar. We even picked up a waitress! So, have at it!"

Monica said, "Waitress, I'm a sous chef."

"What's a taco?" Serena asked.

Magda picked her up and talked to her, "Let me introduce you to the best food on this planet. The idea is that you make it the way you want it. If you like something a lot, add more. If you dislike something, don't add it to your taco. Come on, let's go make a practice taco."

Everyone watched and waited as Magda led Serena through the process: the meats, the vegetables, the sauces, and the toppings. They sat at a table, and everyone watched. Magda showed her how to eat it so nothing spilled out.

"I like this! This is good, Auntie M," Serena said. It was the first time she called her Auntie, but Magda liked it.

Everyone ate till they were full.

Mik told the room, "There are a lot of leftovers, so we can make Huevos Rancheros or a taco scramble for breakfast. If anyone gets hungry during the night, it's all in the fridge."

~~~~~~~~~~

Marissa asked, "Who gets what room?"

Virginia handed out the room assignments. Everyone had a room except for Serena. "I wondered if you were going to sleep. Let's see, I can put a sleeping pad on the floor in your parent's room, or you can share the room across the hall from them with me. I have an extra bed in my room."

Serena looked at her Mom, then at Virginia. "Mommy, can I have a sleepover with Aunt V?"

"You can. Just remember you both need to sleep."

"Yes, Mommy." She turned to Virginia, "I think your room. I'm a big girl now."

"Excellent. Got pajamas?" Virginia asked.

"No, I forgot them."

"Let's see if we can find something for you to sleep in." They walked to the other end of the building, a huge closet, and she found a tiny pair of fleece pants and a long-sleeved shirt of the same material. It showed a pair of fuzzy gray kittens on the front. Virginia grabbed a similar set but a single cat with long white fur.

She went into her parents' room to show them and came out wearing the bedclothes. Virginia had also changed and found a pair of slippers to fit her little feet. They looked like sisters. In reality, Virginia and Rory were not all that much older than Marshall and Ramona. So, an older sister or aunt was very plausible.

Virginia showed her how to use the bed and the sleeping bag but told her there was no need to zip it up in the building. Just use it like a floppy blanket. Serena lay in her bed and was sound asleep in minutes.

Virginia walked out to the common area where Brigit and Ramona were sitting.

"She passed out fast!" Virginia said.

"That trip took a lot out of her," Ramona said. "I feel it myself, but I love talking to my favorite aunt."

"I had another vision about the community," Brigit said.

"So did I. In my vision, you were in the square, in your car. The car Rory and Marcel used to get dinner."

"I had a similar vision, but in mine, I landed in the community, and when I got to the building, you were there to greet me. Serena and her husband came in, and all three of you wore the necklace."

Ramona said, "But with the community, how can it be that my entire family sits, or will sit, on the council of elders?"

"The impression I felt in the vision was that the council would change from how it is now to those with the gift of visions. My parents were powerful and strong, as were yours. You are stronger than your parents, and your daughter is our strongest to date. You and I need concentration and seclusion, but Serena Brigit, it is like an afterthought. It just happens. Her husband will have a gift similar to Joseph, and one day, they will take over our positions once Magda retires or moves on. Virginia will take her place one day after Mik retires."

"Magda will die on a trip to Neptune. I have seen it." Ramona said, "There is nothing that can be done. It is decades from now and will be both painless and fast. She called it an aneurysm. She remained on the ship until Brigit found her. They speak briefly until she realizes she can be anywhere. She visited you on Earth before she moved on. My mother came to get her."

"So I will see her one last time to say goodbye. And I will get to see Serena again, too?"

"Yes to both questions," Ramona said.

Virginia cleared her throat, "I'm sitting right here. But I do have a question: who called it an aneurysm?"

"Oh, sorry." They both said.

Brigit added, "Magda's spirit."

Virginia added, "Really?" She paused less than a heartbeat, "So, a few decades from now, I will be a general running this group. The boss will die peacefully in a shuttle heading to Neptune alone, and Brigit will locate her remains and bring them home."

Brigit said, "You and I will head to find her, and we do. Thanks to this little conversation we are having right now. It is all already set into motion. It is going to happen." Ramona looked at Brigit and nodded as she spoke, "Yes. But you can not ever mention it to anyone. Do you understand? If someone hears it, it may not happen, and things may change. Not a good thing."

"So, this gift of yours may be all cool and great, but it seems like it is seriously a pain in the ass!"

Ramona and Brigit added emphatically, "YES, Definitely!"

Brigit added, "I know things about everyone," Ramona nodded in agreement, "And as such, I cannot tell them, or anyone for that matter, what I know."

Virginia asked, "Things like what?"

Brigit said, "Rory and Marcel will be married, have three children, live well past 100 years, and eventually take over the farm from Joseph and me. In a decade, the community will join the universe fully, cars will land in the square, and the small buildings that pop up will become shops and stores, and they will trade for items. People around the solar system will consider the settlement a spa or a vacation destination. My ultimate return to the community as a visitor with the newcomers from the station will be to land my car in the square to introduce the community to what is really out there. I know how and close to when Joseph will die. I cannot say anything to him since he will worry about it, and it will create bad judgment in his future ventures."

"Wow!" Virginia said.

"That's not a small part of it all. When I meet someone and shake their hands or look deep into their eyes, I see their entire life unfold as it will unfold," she said. She walked to Virginia and extended her hand. Virginia grabbed it, and Ramona froze for a moment. A second later, she returned and smiled at Virginia.

"So, what did you see?" Virginia asked.

"A wonderful, amazing, fulfilled life complete with friends and family. I saw you receive awards, commendations, and promotions. Rory's son and daughter will work for you one day, and they will call you Aunt General as a loving joke. I also know you will live well past 100, and your death will be peaceful and silent."

"Damn!" Virginia said, "I'm not sure I wanted to know all that."

"Welcome to my life!" Brigit said.

"Mine too," Ramona said.

"Oh dear!" Ramona exclaimed.

"Virginia, do not say anything. Just get Mik and Monica, NOW!" Brigit said.

Virginia stood and ran to their room.

"Hi, Mik. Do you know where you are?" Brigit said.

"Well, seriously. I know I'm no longer one of the living. I was at my funeral, and wait, you can see me?" Mik Sr. said.

"I can, and so can my niece Ramona."

"WHAT!" Mik ran into the room.

"Uh, Mik. Remember how I saw Brad and talked to him?"

"Yes, where's this heading?"

"Your Dad's here. Usually, that means they are ready to move on, but I am sure he would love a conversation with you and Monica."

"Wow! Nice outfit!" Mik Sr said. Brigit started laughing.

"What?" Mik said.

"Your Dad said, Nice Outfit," Brigit said to him.

Monica walked in, "What's going on?"

Mik told his wife, "Evidently, my Dad is in the room and thinks I am well dressed."

Monica laughed until the reality of what he said hit her, and she stopped laughing like someone flipped a switch.

Mik Sr. said, "Tell Monica she forgot to turn off the stockroom light, but that's not a big deal. Tell her the store has been doing great since she took it over. I also know that a man will be there tomorrow and wants everything. He heard about the store being for sale, but the biggest thing he needs to acquire for a mining company is the rocks. Before you sell it, there is one rock you need to mine. It is packed full of a diamond as big as Brigit's car and a blob of gold that has never been seen in history. Oh, and tell her that behind the painting in the office is a small safe. She must open that safe before they sell the metal shop and all its assets and empty it out."

Brigit passed on what Mik was saying.

"I know about the safe, but I don't know the code." She said. "I had station maintenance look at it, but they cannot cut into it without damaging the integrity of the structure of the station."

"Tell her the safe code is 6-4-4-5-4-6-7-7-5-8." Brigit wrote it down, "6/4/45 was my wife's birthday. 467758 was the tag number to my first car." He laughed a little, "In the safe are rare minerals and gemstones I found over the years, plus a deed to a plot of land on the Moon I bought when his mother was still alive. We planned to build and live there when we retired." She passed on the information he had said.

"Dad. How are you?" Mik said.

"I'm dead! But overall, I feel pretty good."

Brigit and Ramona started laughing.

"What?" Monica said.

"He still has his sense of humor. He said, his words exactly, I'm dead! But overall, I feel pretty good." Virginia started laughing, like Mik. Monica looked a little freaked out but smiled.

Ramona spoke, "Mik Sr told you to pull up a chart of the belt, and he will tell you which rocks you need to grab."

Mik did, and his Dad's spirit walked to the screen and pointed. Ramona touched the rocks he pointed to, and the system flagged them for later examination. Mik was messaging the mining team and told them to focus on these specific rocks for the next month. They will get a 45% commission, more than twice the standard commission if they do.

"Dad, I just offered the team a 45% commission on those rocks. How much are we talking?"

Brigit spoke for him, "He said that those four rocks should pull in about 9 million, so those guys should get about a million each, and Mik and Monica about five million."

"DAMN!" Monica said.

"There's more out there, too, not just these; it's just that these are the fastest and easiest to get, mine, and sell. Brigit, what's that?" Mik Sr said.

"What's what? She replied.

Serena Brigit came into the room. "Hi, Mr. Mik. I thought you had moved on already."

"No, kid. But what is that light?"

Serena replied before the others could, "That is your portal to the next. All you need to do is touch it, and you will be moved on. Go ahead, give it a try."

"Does it hurt?" Mik Sr. said, and Serena laughed.

"No, some say it feels nice, like a warm hug."

"Well, tell my kid I love him and that crazy wife of his. Those two are perfect for each other. Yin and Yang."

Mik Sr. walked to the light and touched it, "It does feel like a warm hug," a moment later, he vanished.

Monica, Ramona, Brigit, and Mik had tears in their eyes. Serena asked them, "Why are you all so sad and crying?"

"We will miss Mr. Mik," Monica said.

"Don't be sad. He'll be back again with his new body."

Monica said, "His new body?"

"Yes. Once you move on, you get a new body in the new place. Michael has a new body, and we talk once in a while. He gets to visit me when they let him. Why did he call you Yin and Yang?" She turned, "I am going back to bed, Aunt V. Are you coming too?"

"In a few minutes, kiddo," Virginia said.

"OK, can you tuck me in when you get there?" She left the room and headed back to bed.

Virginia looked at Ramona, "How old is this kid again? 40?" She smiled at Ramona. "For such a youngin, she is quite mature and understanding."

Brigit replied, "It comes with the gift. You see many things and have many experiences before you really know what you are seeing and experiencing. She'll be fine."

Brigit asked, "Who's Michael?"

"He was a boy close to her age. He died of some illness about a year ago. He was in my house more after he died than before. He liked to have me tell his Mom things, but I could no longer see or hear him after he moved on. However, Serena seems able to see and talk to people who have moved on, like my mother. She shows up once in a while."

"You people are strange. Cool, but strange," Virginia said, "OK, I need to shut down my cranial computer. Good night."

Virginia left the room, and Brigit and Ramona talked a little longer and then went to bed. Since they were the last to go to bed, they hit the lights as they left the room.

Brigit undressed and crawled into bed with Joseph.

"What was the commotion?"

"Mik Sr showed up to say hello before he moved on."

"He's moving on, wonderful. What did he have to say?"

"He gave Monica the code to the hidden safe in the office and touched the light."

"Excellent."

"He also gave them the location of a few asteroids that will rake in several million dollars in profit."

"Fantastic. Good night."

"Good night, my love," She pulled the covers close and tight and fell asleep fast. While she was sleeping, she dreamt about finding Magda's shuttle with her dead in the pilot seat. She did have a conversation with her spirit in her dream and remembered the coordinates where she found the shuttle.

It seems that it was on manual and headed to Neptune. When she died, it just kept going. She looked at the velocity indicator and saw it was 50% power, so it would be easy to catch up to when the time came. Docking would be interesting at that speed, but she had also thought about that. She noticed the date and time when she looked at the console. She knows where she needs to be and when. She will not tell anyone the date, and Virginia and Ramona understand that the event will occur but not precisely when, so she will need to remind Virginia about it when it happens.

~~~~~~~~~~

The group got up early, at 4:30am, and had breakfast and cleaned the kitchen. Brigit walked to Virginia and said quietly, "Remember what we talked about last night?" She nodded, "You can never speak about it to anyone, and in a few decades, I will walk into your office and say NEPTUNE. Nothing else. You need to call and prep your shuttle, as you and I will leave at that time to retrieve the wayward shuttle. As I already said, no one can ever know about this."

"I understand," she said, "But I have a question. Will I get married? Will I be happy in the romance department?"

Brigit froze. When she moved again, "You will, you are."

Virginia was about to speak, but Brigit said, "He is a fine male specimen, too!" She laughed, as did Virginia. She was about to ask when they would meet or where, but Brigit held up a finger, "No more info. When it happens, it happens."

Magda said as they approached the group, "Secret meeting?"

Virginia and Brigit said, "Yep!"

Ramona said, "OK, everyone. They will be here in 15 minutes, landing in the clearing down the hill. I think setting up a few chairs outside at the head of the trail with Mik, Magda, Marissa, and Brigit would be our best option. When they break through the trees, they will see you, be shocked, and wonder what you are doing here. You need to state this exactly to them."

She paused momentarily and said, "As per order X33576, you were to covertly explore an unknown settlement in the mountains roughly 100 miles away. Your orders have been rescinded, and your new assignment is per order X33576A."

"What are the new orders," Magda asked.

"No idea, but I assume you will make them up on the spot to fit the situation. The temperature will be 20°F when they arrive, and you can invite them in for breakfast since none of them had the chance to eat this morning."

"Good to know."

"The four investigators all like waffles, maple syrup, butter, grits, link sausage, soft scrambled eggs, coffee, and orange juice." Mik said, "Monica and Ramona will head to the kitchen and prep a good breakfast for them. Then, we four can sit and wait for them to emerge from the trees."

Magda gave a thumbs-up, walked into the kitchen, grabbed a coffee for each of them, and returned to where her chair was waiting for her. The rest of the group went into the kitchen and waited.

Ramona looked at the clock, "One minute and they will be there." Monica looked out the window and saw them all sitting there. Four people and a grav cart emerged from the trees a minute later. They were all talking now.

"They're here. They just appeared; it is 0600, so good vision, Ramona," Monica said.

~~~~~~~~~~

"Well, hello," Magda said as the four walked through the trees and out on the path to the cave. They had no idea a hoteling system was set up, nor did they know that two people in this group they were about to meet were from the settlement they were sent to investigate.

"Hello!" The man said, a little alarmed. People were just sitting and waiting for them to appear.

"I am General MagdaLynne Rochavarro."

"I am Dr. Russ Miyaga. Wait, did you say General Rochavarro?"

"I did."

"I know you, or I know of you. My boss mentioned he was friends with you the other day, and he had a meeting with you."

"Is your boss the Admiral?"

"Yes, Admiral Russell."

"He and I have recently become friends, and I will continue to back him in his endeavors," She paused a moment, "Allow me to introduce my team or a part of it. This is my second in command, Lieutenant Colonel Mik Spencer. Next to him is Brigit Markz, a member of the community you have arrived to investigate; however, she left that community about five years ago to work for me. Our last introduction is Marissa Taylor. She and Brigit are members of the ruling council, referred to internally as the Elders. The others from the community and my team are making your breakfast in the kitchen building. I understand you all are getting hungry."

"We are. We were talking about that on the flight from the station. None of us had the chance to eat anything this morning." He paused momentarily, "As I said, I am Russ Miyaga, team leader, and this is MY second in command, Carole Luccia. Carole is the historical expert on the timeframe in which the settlement appears to be living. This is our resident psychologist, Donald Barr. He is here to evaluate us, them, me, you, the animals he happens across, whatever. The last member of our little group is Ronald Luchinski. We have a job. He has a profession. He is our security specialist. His role is to keep us safe."

Mik asked, "Safe from what?" He smiled at Ronald.

Ronald replied, "Safe from them, you, us, the animals in the woods, the weather, hunger, starvation, dehydration."

Mik and Ronald nodded to each other. Magda saw, and they had mutual respect.

"Luchinski," Magda said, "By chance, are you Margo and Rogers bouncing baby boy?"

"Yes, General. Those are my parents. I take it you know them?"

"I do. As a captain, I worked for your Dad. As a Colonel, I was under your Mom. I love them both to death, by the way. Best bosses in the universe."

Mik added, "Aside from you, Boss!" Magda laughed, and Ronald understood the relationship. "OK, let's head in the building and get you people some breakfast. If you had your choice, what would you want for breakfast?"

Russ said, "Definitely, French Toast."

Mik said, "Maple syrup and butter?"

"Definitely."

Carole said, "I'd love some good, creamy grits."

Mik replied, "Ah! Love me some cheese grits," She agreed.

Donald added, "Scrambled eggs are my fave. Scrambled with cheese would be perfect.

Ronald added his two cents, "I guess I'm the carnivore. What they said is great, but I need some meat. I am a fan of the little link sausages, and if you have maple syrup, I can cover them with, all the better."

Magda said, "Here we are, gang. Let's go inside and grab some food and coffee. By the way, this is your building. There are four rooms down that hall, one for each of you. Pick one and take up residence. But that can wait till after you refuel your tank."

Magda or Mik introduced everyone in the room, and little Serena came running in, "HI. I'm Serena Brigit. That's my Mommy," She pointed to Ramona, "That's my Aunt Brigit, my Aunt V, and my Auntie M," Pointing to Brigit, Virginia, and Magda in order.

Magda defined where people were from for the newcomers, and they were amazed. These two groups of people, unique and diverse, were friends and worked together to keep the secret. Magda continued, "And this smart little lady is Serena…"

"Auntie M, I am Serena Brigit. My name is from my mommy's mommy and her sister," she pointed to Brigit. "She has the gift like Mommy and Grampa and me."

"Oh, I am so sorry mini-kid. Everyone is Serena Brigit. She is instrumental in the fact we are here waiting for you to brief you on the community you are planning to visit and to tell you why that is not a good idea."

Russ asked, "The gift?"

"We will tell you about that briefly, but first, you need FOOD and preliminary information."

Mik took over, "AH! The food. I must let you know that Ramona and Monica are the best sous chefs in this building!" Everyone laughed at that comment, and Ronald asked a question.

"Ahhhhhh, Mik, my new friend. If they are the sous chefs, then who…"

"…..is the chef? Well, I would hate to blow my horn here, but…"

Monica quickly added, "There is no ACTUAL chef, but instead, there is a gaggle of sous chefs, with Ramona and me and my favorite husband, Mik, as part three of this three-part cooking harmony."

Ronald winked at Monica, "If you need a fourth, feel free to draft me. I love kitchen work. I find it relaxing."

Mik said, "Oh good, someone to help me with the dishes!" The room laughed. They quickly became friends, which was the intent of all this pointed back-and-forth fun.

Ramona said, "We have freshly prepared French Toast with maple syrup and melted butter for breakfast."

Monica added, "We also have a pot of cheese grits, and there is enough for all of us to have thirds. I went a little crazy."

"There are enough link sausages to make anyone in this room happy," Mik said, winking at Ronald. "And last, there are the freshest, fluffiest scrambled eggs you will get nowhere else in the universe. If you so desire, I can melt some cheese on the eggs if that is your choice."

Magda took over, "Now, get breakfast, and the briefing will begin. I need to make a few phone calls, and we can get started."

She walked outside and into the other building. She needed to conference with several generals and admirals above and below her, so she used the large screen in the common room of the next building. They talked for ten minutes and agreed to come for lunch."

Walking into the building, "OH, Sous Chefs. There will be five more for lunch. What are we having?"

Virginia said, "I was thinking chili. Medium, mild spice level with additives and cornbread."

The room agreed.

Virginia said, "I'll start it shortly."

Mik added, "The Sous Chef Trio will assist."

Ronald said, "Quartet?" Mik and the women nodded in agreement.

Virginia gave a thumbs up.

Magda started speaking, "OK, you all go grab chow. I will start talking." She glanced up at the clock on the wall above the door. Ten minutes till 7, "Let's start this briefing at 7. I figure we can get it all done well before lunch and open it to questions from the floor. Besides, that French Toast smells amazing, and I had breakfast several hours ago."

Ramona opened the left oven and removed 4 trays of French Toast. Perfectly hot and ready to eat. Monica went to the right oven and set up the sausages and a hotel pan of scrambled eggs.

Monica added, "If scrambled aren't your cup of tea, we can make you a couple over easy or whatever."

No one wanted made-to-order eggs, so everyone went through the line, grabbed what they wanted, refilled their coffee, and found a seat to eat and listen to the lecture. They all had a paper pad and a pen to jot down notes or questions. Rory and Marcel saw to that as they handed them out to everyone when Magda made her phone call.

Magda made a plate, ate it fast, and sipped a coffee. "OK. Listen up. We need to get this briefing on the road."

She looked around the room and started talking, "OK, my two cents," Magda said, "The community is filled with just under 500 people ranging in age from less than a year old to 70."

"Make that 76," Marissa added.

"OK, 76. They have basic electricity, a deep freeze walk-in, and all the amenities in their homes like they were in the late 1800s. So, lamp and candle for interior light, cooking on a fire in a cast iron stove, and internal heating during the winter is a fireplace in as many rooms in the home as can be safely accommodated."

She paused and sipped her coffee, "Mik and Rory, please come up here and give us your impression of the community during your visit a couple of years ago."

They stood and walked to the front of the room.

~~~~~~~~~~~

They broke for lunch, and the investigation team found their rooms. The idea of the gifts was discussed during the question and answer period. Ramona and Brigit explained it as best as they could.

Ramona walked over to Russ and extended her hand. He was a little leary to offer his hand in return because she had already told them all that if she shook hands with someone, she saw things in their future.

Russ held hands with Ramona, and she froze. A few seconds later, she started up again and looked at him.

"Before I say anything, do you want me to say it?"

He thought about it briefly and asked, "Is anything embarrassing?"

"No." She replied.

"Then spill the beans!"

Ramona said, "OK. You will take a vacation trip to the Mars colony with your wife in a few months to celebrate your 10th anniversary. While there, you will find ways to work, and she will not be happy. An argument will happen, and the next few days are not fun, but finally, you make up and spend the last two days happily. My suggestion is not to find ways to work. It seems your work is taking a front seat in your car now, and your wife is not happy about it, but she doesn't want to say anything to you. Be there for her. If you do, that child you have waited for for eight years will be conceived on this trip. A girl, happy and healthy and born on my birthday, October 1."

"Do you know her name?" He asked.

"I do, but you and your wife will make that decision when you make that decision."

He nodded and started to go back to his seat and thanked her. They shook hands again, and Ramona got another vision.

"I just saw that you will get a call this afternoon. You need to take it immediately. It is from your brother; his wife and son will be injured and hospitalized. Nothing you can do about it now, nor anytime this week. They will be in an induced coma for six days, and you will be there when his wife," Ramona concentrated for the name, "Madelynne, comes out of it. She will tell you where you were last week. She will know about this conversation and ask you about the community. You will know what you need to say to her at that moment. Please remember that when this team completes its mission, you must put your family differences aside and be with your brother and his other children. You can be the cool uncle, as his middle son will call you. Your relationship with your family will mend, and you will become a family again," She laughed briefly. Everyone looked at her, wondering, "Sorry, you will all be together at his house next winter holiday, your brothers. You will assist him in cooking, and may I recommend taking a cooking class beforehand. You and your brother burn the turkey pretty bad, too, and you end up making meatloaf. You laugh about it, and the meatloaf becomes a new family tradition."

The room was laughing at what would happen. Carole put her hand up.

Ramona asked, "Yes, Carole, you have a question?"

"I do. How do I know this is all the truth? What you 'SEE' is what will happen? For example, all of these things you envision are so far in the future; they may or may not happen, but will we even care by then."

At that moment, Serena returned. She walked up to Carole and stopped, staring at her. "Your phone is going to ring. Your daughter will tell you she is having a baby, their first child. It will be a boy, and they will name him William, after your husband, who died a few months ago." Without saying another word, she left the room and returned to wherever she was playing.

"What was that about?" Carole asked.

"I suppose that it is a vision specifically for you to allow you to open your mind to the possibilities." Carole's phone rang.

"Hello…. Yes Marina, OH MY, that is wonderful…. Have you thought of names?" She paused, "I love it. I'm in a meeting at the moment. I'll call you back later this evening. Give my love to Bruce." She hung up. She looked at everyone, "The kid is good. OK, you got a believer in me." She paused momentarily, "How can I, I mean WE, help?"

They talked for another hour, and the guests started arriving.

CHAPTER ELEVEN

The past few days have been an eye-opening experience. Ramona and Marshall brought Russ and Carole back to the settlement where they observed.

They had a recording device, but it was cleverly concealed in a shoulder bag carried by Carole and a small pack carried by Russ.

They spent the night at Ramona's home, visited many people and places around the community, and learned a great deal about these people and their lifestyles.

Carole had a wonderful time in the community until someone asked her about her home village. They saw the truth, as Marshall does, and realized something was wrong. Marshall pulled him aside and explained the truth, more or less. He was satisfied with the explanation, and they went to have dinner.

Entering the house, Ramona closed the door, and they sat in the living room.

"This house was built by Brigit and her first husband, Brad," Ramona told them.

Russ asked, "The man killed by the bear attack and the one who watched Marcel and his group map the planet?"

"Yes," Marshall said, "Who's hungry?" His and three other hands went up.

Ramona told them, "Food is pretty simple here. Meat, bread, a vegetable or two, coffee or tea, or if you prefer, plain water."

"I had something a few months ago that I have been perfecting in my kitchen," Marshall said, "Who likes beef stroganoff?"

Everyone nodded.

"Well, not exactly beef, but really good," He said.

"Uh," Carole spoke, "Not exactly beef?"

"No, eating cows is not good for the community. A few each year are raised for the table, and the remainder are for milk. This is a veal stroganoff."

They stared at him, and he continued, "Veal, young cows, are abundant at a specific time of the year. If every cow in the community gave birth, they would outnumber the people in no time. Therefore, to maintain a balance, we need to thin the herd, so to speak. When we do, that calf is processed and placed in the freezer. Anyone in the community can remove meat from the freezer when needed. Some shop daily when to gather what they need for the next day. During the winter, every household is encouraged to retain at least several days, if not a week, to feed their family."

There was a knock at the door.

Marshall stood and walked to the door. He opened it, "Elder Carpenter. Welcome."

"Hello, Marshall, Ramona. I hear we have guests from…. another village."

"We do. Please come in and join us. I was about to make dinner for us all, and one more plate means I will not have leftovers."

"You are an odd character, son. But I like you anyway."

~~~~~~~~~~

Serena Brigit stayed at the cave site; they referred to her as their mascot, and everyone spent some time with her. The two from the investigation team sat with her. They drew on paper until they realized she was drawing a space station currently in the planning and early construction phases, but it was completed in her drawing. She is a talented artist, and the colorations and shadows made it an impressive station.

Donald asked, "What are you drawing, little one?"

"Your new house."

"My new house?"

"Yes, your wife will get asked to run the science team there, and you will move there. You will live here," She pointed to the largest ring, a set of windows.

Donald asked her, "Is this a good move for our family?"

Serena Brigit paused, "It is. You all think it is great. You tell them every day it is the best view in the universe. But a year after you move there you will get sick. The doctors can't figure it out until you tell them about something that your Daddy had when he was a kid. Then they fix you all up," She drew a little more, then said, "Your daughter is beautiful, too."

"I don't have any children," He said, not quite out loud but loud enough. The reality hit him, and he kissed Serena lightly on her head.

As he kissed her, the physical connection was made, and she saw something else, "Oh, after they make you all better, tell your wife she needs to check the baffle plates of the shuttle she will fly to Neptune station."

"What happens if she forgets to check the baffle plates?"

"Bad things."

~~~~~~~~~~~

After breakfast, Russ called the rest of his team, and Ramona contacted Brigit. Over the past few years, Elder Carpenter was made the lead Elder of the committee. His leadership and guidance have brought them closer to the current technology, but they are still worlds away. His wife, Mel or Melinda, saw it one night in a dream that he would be the one to bring the community into the future.

Without Brigit, her trusted confidant, she did not know who to talk to about the visions and told David what she saw. When David traveled the last time, he knew this was a part of the vision, and he began the process, slow as it needed to be, to enlighten the community. He set in motion certain fuzes that could not be extinguished once lit. Brigit and Joseph are two of the significant figures in these fuzes.

The trip to the cave took less than 5 hours, and David Carpenter made the trip with them. David needed to begin to have a real trade team, and he planned to name Ramona and Marshall as the leaders and the chairs for the required items. This would supplement the collection if possible, but not replace it.

As they arrived at the cave, Marshall and Joseph took the cart and settled the horses into their temporary barn.

Brigit saw David and went up and gave him a huge hug. They had not seen each other in several years. David said quietly to her, "We need to talk. Mel dreamed about you, them, us, and what will happen to the community."

Brigit replied, "As did Ramona and me. We will discuss it shortly. But for now, come in and have lunch with us," She asked David, "How is your wife? Mel has the same gift as Ramona and I."

"And her daughter, I understand," He said quickly.

"True."

They went into the building and the kitchen area, and the others all saw David and bid him hello, a handshake, or a hug.

~~~~~~~~~~

David spent a few days with the teams. He believes the only way to keep the community intact is to show the community what is out there and let them understand they are vital to the community.

Mik and David took Brigit's car and headed to the station. Mik had a video of the entire trip. He took David to the moon, and they flew over the colonies and the stations and then back to the cave. He called and spoke to Biff, asked him to do a high-level pass over the colony, and asked him to send the video. It took an hour, but the video made it to him before he returned to the cave area.

They arrived back the following morning exhausted, but an understanding was made. David needed to ease the community into the future and the future into the community.

Mik sent the video to Virginia, as did Biff, who cut and edited it into a logical progression. Total length: an hour. It showed everything in orbit, the moon's surface and Mars's domes and stations. As Virginia edited it together, she had images of a beautiful full Earth shrinking to a dot and a beautiful red ball; Mars, growing as the view approached the planet, traveled near the stations and descended to the primary and two secondary communities of Mars. The video ended with a view of the Earth, a slow zoom into the community, and a final stop at the council building. She also added the drone footage that Russ gave her. Russ asked for a copy of the finished video because it was exceptionally well made and will highlight his report.

Everyone watched the video in silence. Mik made a massive batch of popcorn and served a variety of drinks. Serena enjoyed the video, and when it focused on the settlement, she yelled that she had seen her house.

"Virginia," David said, "That is beyond words. It is informative, spellbinding, mesmerizing, and beautiful. You did a fantastic job assembling the video, and I hope I can do it justice."

He applauded, as did everyone else in the room. Serena jumped up and hopped into her lap, and she gave her a big hug.

David spoke to the group assembled and let them all know that the members of the Council of Elders will be updated. Four will have the vision, two will have the animal gift, and one will have discernment. David and Marissa have discernment, as in the human lie detector. His wife, Mel, Mark, and Ramona have the vision. Marshall and Louise have the animal gift. That makes eight, but at the moment, Mel is not on the council.

Russ asked during dinner, "David. What will the repercussions be if Brigit and Joseph walk into the settlement?"

"I have thought about that," He said, "And came up with a solution. A few days after I return, after all of us return, I will hold several informational sessions where the video Mik and I took, and Virginia edited so well, will be played, explained, and understood by those in the community. The goal is to bring the community to understand that the rest of the universe lives differently than we do, but not better."

Magda added quickly, "You got that right!"

"Therefore," David continued, "After all community members are informed, understand, and are 'good' with the idea, I will contact Mik and Rory to arrive in a ground car to bring something we need. A day later, Virginia, Brigit, Joseph, and you, Magda, can land in the square in Brigit's car."

Ramona and Brigit froze momentarily, and when they unfroze, "David, I had a vision that the community would be fine with what you said. I see that a few want to leave the community to explore the rest of the planet and do so."

"I saw this also," Ramona said, "Several worldwide would like to become a community member. People who have no urge to collect wealth or work for no other reason than to work. They need a purpose."

Serena walked in, looking like a zombie. She walked up to David and stopped in front of him. Her eyes were pure white. When she spoke, it was not her voice, but it was.

"Uncle David, I have seen the results of your intervention and merging of the worlds. I know the community will remain and thrive. A new council position will be as liaison to the universe. The person's primary role is to vet requests to join or leave the community. Ramona, my mother, and Aunt Marissa are the best people for this role. Together, they will maintain the colony's duties, responsibilities, and integrity. Auntie M will provide tiny houses that can be used for this purpose. As community members depart, their residence can be reissued to those arriving."

She just turned and walked back down the hall.

Virginia was sitting on the couch with David when Serena entered and did her thing.

"OK, is that normal?"

Everyone from the community said, "NO!"

Virginia stood and went to find Serena. She was in their room playing on the floor with some toy, a doll she had brought with her.

"Hi, Kiddo! How are you?"

"I'm good, Aunt V." She held up the doll, "Do you know Dolly?"

"I don't, is she your baby?"

"She is. I like playing with her a lot," She turned to the side a moment and laughed, "I did?"

"Did what?" Virginia asked.

"Aunt V, did I go in the big room and tell Uncle David something?"

"Yes, you did. You don't remember?"

"No, Michael told me what I did. Did I do something wrong?"

"Oh, no, not at all. You helped everyone understand what needed to be done. They are talking about it right now," She got a chill, "Is Michael in the room?"

"He was. He came in with you. He said I can trust you, so I call you Aunt V. Besides, one day, I will work with you like Aunt Brigit."

"I am looking forward to that day, kiddo. When you work for me, can I still call you kiddo, or do I need to call you Miss Serena?"

She thought for a minute, then jumped up and hugged Virginia, "When we are alone, call me kiddo. But when others are around, it may be better to call me Serena."

Virginia hugged her back and said, "You got it, KIDDO!"

~~~~~~~~~~~

Serena Brigit opened her eyes. The room was pretty dark, and she was lying on her bed across from Virginia, who was sound asleep. Without thinking about it, she crawled into bed with Virginia. Serena touched Virginia's head with her finger:

> *Serena walked into the general's office a bit earlier than usual. She was alone for the moment. The general should be here in the next half hour. She activated the screen and trained the scanner on the colony.*
>
> *She stood and walked to the dispenser; she needed a cup of coffee. Grabbing her cup, the cup her mother gave her*

all those years ago, she filled it with coffee.

Walking back to the console, she looked at the window. The stars and the Earth were beautiful this morning. She saw her reflection and realized again that she looked like her mother and grandmother.

"Hey, Kiddo, you do look like your mother," Virginia said as she entered the room.

"Aunt General," using the name Rory's kids call her, "You're in the office early?"

"I am. I have a meeting at Jupiter Station later this evening, so I'll spend the night. By the way, do you want to go with me? I know you like Jupiter Station. Last time, Michael was there and told you where all the fun stuff was, right?"

"Yes, I see Michael less and less as I get older. Mr. Mik was here when I arrived this

morning. He said hello. He will be gone for a while. He and a few others are heading to other solar systems to see what's there. Funny how no one has done that yet. I asked Michael about it, and he said the transfer there takes a lot out of them and takes months. Really boring, he said."

"Good to know," She thought momentarily, "Office, call Rory."

A moment later, "GV, to what do I owe the pleasure?"

"I'm heading to Jupiter, taking Serena with me. Wanna go with us, girls trip?"

"Sorry, got stuff to do. When Gayle passed away a few years ago, Jon asked Marcel and me to help with his farm. Last year, when he passed, we found out he gave us the farm, and since then, Marcel

and I have been occupied. Take my babies with you. It'll be fun. Besides, Serena can keep you from getting into trouble."

After a bit more small talk, they disconnected. Serena calculated the life in the community, and a few seconds later, she saw it was the same as when she left last night. Looking at the schedule, she saw that a few transports were due to trade.

Brigit walked into the office and stood just inside the doorway. She looked at Virginia until they locked eyes. Brigit said a single word, "Neptune."

Virginia scrunched her face, trying to understand the reference to Neptune. Her eyes opened wide a second later, and she remembered their conversation nearly 20 years ago. They needed to go retrieve Magda, who died of an aneurysm in the shuttle heading for Neptune yesterday.

She pressed a button on her desk, "Cancel everything for the next few days, ready my shuttle for immediate launch. Classified trip, two souls on board."

Not saying a word, Serena raised her hand and held up three fingers.

"Make it three souls. We depart in 30 minutes." She disconnected before the bay could acknowledge.

Brigit had an overnight bag. Since the new ships were made of new material, there was no longer a need to wear a pressure suit in the shuttle. They are carried, though, but only worn when needed.

Serena looked at the upper left of the console. She noted the day and time and logged it into her memory.

They had been traveling to Neptune at full speed, maybe an hour and a half.

"Hi, Jon," Brigit said.

"Hi, Uncle Jon," Serena said, "Can you go find Auntie M?"

A few minutes later, he returned, "She is near death, a matter of minutes, actually. Very peaceful and no pain at all."

"Thanks, Jon. Go be with her until we arrive."

Virginia said, "10 minutes to the coordinates."

They arrived, and Virginia went to the pilot's seat. She still had a pulse. A moment later, it stopped. "She's gone."

"But I did not die alone, thank you all," Magda said.

"Auntie M, you know that you died?"

"I do, kid. I also know I can talk to the two of you. How does this work?"

"We have no idea. It just does. When you see the light, touch it. When you do, you will move on."

They moved Magda's remains to the passenger area, stretching her onto the floor. She looked at peace.

Brigit sat in the pilot's seat and switched on the comm.

"Neptune Station, this is Brigit Markz in Shuttle 3723; I am declaring an emergency."

"Hi Brigit, please define the emergency?"

"Retired General MagdaLynne Rochavarro has died. We are bringing her to Neptune Station."

"Understood. You are cleared for a straight-in approach, bay 1. Our

*thoughts are with you and
her friends and family."*

*"Thank you, Tony. ETA is 9
minutes."*

~~~~~~~~~~~

Roughly a minute later, Virginia started crying.
She grabbed Serena Brigit and held her tight,
"Oh my god, kiddo. Is that how it happens?"

"Yes, Aunt V. But it is OK. Auntie M will be
fine after and move on fast because her life has
been for others."

Virginia looked at the clock. It was 5:12 am.
Today, everyone is heading home. "We may as
well get up and make coffee."

"Yes, good plan. I will like coffee when I get
older."

"Maybe I can make you something my daddy
made me as a kid. Coffee milk. You want to try
it?"

Serena nodded, and they dressed to start the day.

Virginia set up the coffee pot, which was more
of a large urn and ready to drink in a few
minutes. She poured herself a cup, then made
Serena a coffee milk. "OK, let's see if I
remember it right. Half a cup of milk, sugar, and
a little vanilla, then coffee."

She stirred it all together and handed it to Serena. The cups matched. Serena mentioned that she loved the milk from the coffee.

Ramona walked in, "And what is little miss drinking?" Virginia and Serena looked like that kid caught with his hand in the cookie jar.

Virgina said, "Oh, oh, Kiddo. We're busted!"

"Coffee milk," Serena said.

Ramona stopped and looked at the ceiling, Virginia said, "My Dad used to make them for me when I was 6, so I figured since she is a big girl now…."

Ramona poured herself a cup and sat opposite these two. "Coffee milk. I remember that, too. My Daddy made them for me, too."

"What did I make?" Mark said as he walked into the room.

Serena held up a glass, "Coffee Milk!"

Mark stopped dead in his tracks, "By golly, I remember that. Your mother thought I was nuts giving a six-year-old coffee."

"I thought Virginia was nuts giving a six-year-old coffee until I heard that name and realized it was a good thing."

Virginia said, "Glad that coffee milk is MOM and GRANDPA approved." She finished her cup and said, "I'll get dressed and tend to the horses."

Ramona added, "I'll give you a hand as well."

~~~~~~~~~~

Virginia walked into the kitchen dressed and ready to tend to the horses. "Brigit, Ramona," She said, "I need to speak to you privately."

Virginia looked agitated.

Ramona said, "We were about to help tend to the horses. Would you like to join us?"

"It would be my pleasure," Virginia said, smiling.

They walked into the makeshift barn and shut the door. The wind was biting cold, and they really were not appropriately dressed. In the barn, they refilled the food, made sure the water was topped off, and rinsed the droppings and other things off the floor or, more precisely, to a trough on the far wall. They talked while they worked.

"OK, what's this about?" Ramona asked.

Virginia thought for a moment or two and looked at Ramona, "Little bit did something new. She touched my head while I slept, and I saw the station's vision, Brigit walking in and saying

Neptune, and the three of us, Me, Serena, and Brigit, flying to get Magda. I saw it as you all see it. I saw Jon, who died a year before, appear and tell you where Magda was located, and he stayed with her until she died. We made it and held her hand as she died, and her spirit thanked us for being there with her. We brought her to Jupiter Station, emergency landing, and that's when it ends."

"Who was the controller?" Brigit asked.

"Tony!" she said with a confidence like they had never seen before.

"That's the controller I see when I see the incident," She looked at each of them, "This is new."

Ramona and Brigit started tending to the horses.

"If this is a new gift, the council needs to know. Perhaps as the children of children with the gift evolve, so does the gift," Brigit said. She froze.

"OK, those born in the community can acquire gifts. Those who choose to join the community will not develop a gift naturally. However, in a few years, a method will exist to give a gift through an injection. Ramona, you must let the council know about this, find all with the gift, and talk to them about this."

Ramona said, "Thanks to Rory, I see." She turned to Virginia, "Can I run a test?"

She walked to Virginia and held her hand, and a vision appeared. She let go and touched her head, and the vision appeared to Virginia, but Ramona appeared as though it had taken a lot out of her.

"Cool. Thanks."

"I had no idea I could do this. It opens up a lot of possibilities."

Brigit attempted the same thing, and nothing happened. She saw the vision but was unable to transfer it to Virginia.

They finished the horses and headed back to the kitchen. "We are heading back shortly. But I want to give you a gift," Ramona said to Monica and Mik.

She held their hands simultaneously and said they had a combined and mutual future they would experience together. She let go of their hands and touched them both on the head. A second later, they both grabbed her and thanked her. It was a vision – private and personal – for them alone.

EPILOGUE

It has been over a month, nearly two, since the meeting at the cave, and David has had the opportunity to personally speak to everyone in the settlement. Virginia and Rory were able to come up with a few gifts for the community when they showed up.

As the car pulled into the square in front of Brigit's favorite bench, the snow fell, and the white blanket covering everything made a beautiful, serene, and quiet area. The stillness of the area and the environment added to the reverence and history being marked at this moment. The snow was maybe a foot deep, and it was obvious some people were a bit cold; thankfully, the wind was not blowing. The air temperature was below freezing but not extremely uncomfortable.

Mik and Rory drove the ground car into the settlement and exited the vehicle. No one seemed too shocked, so David explained it to everyone well enough.

David walked out of the council building, "Mik…. Rory….. So nice to see you again. Would you like something hot to drink or maybe something to eat?"

"No, David, we are fine, but a hot beverage does sound wonderful," Mik said, and Rory nodded.

Mik reached into the back seat and removed a rather large box. He asked a few strong lads to assist him, and they, three of them, carried the boxes and placed them onto the steps of the council building.

David turned, "OK, Mik. What is that?"

"Well, you enjoyed our coffee. I thought I would bring you enough for a year. Brew it like you would normally. It is already perfectly roasted and ground."

"What about everyone else?" David asked, already knowing the answer.

Rory jumped up, "Sorry, Sir. There are four of these packages in the backseat. That should be enough for everyone in the community to drink the best coffee on the planet until at least the end of summer."

David started laughing. Mark asked, "Is this the coffee we had during our conference?"

"Better!" Rory said.

"Then definitely count me in!"

They walked into the building, and Marshall and Mark walked up to the car and opened the trunk. "Help us with this, please." They had been briefed that they were the crew to handle this task while David spoke to the two in the building.

They unloaded a few things they could not get in the community. Coats and scarves and gloves. Marshall said, "This is Magda's winter gear," Mik nodded. The items all appear like typical attire in the community with one exception: the community logo, the logo on the exterior wall of the council building, and the necklace worn by council members is a patch sewn to the upper left of each item and on the scarves and gloves.

As they entered, people stared at them. One man said, "You look familiar."

Rory stopped, "Got enough wood for your fireplace?"

"AH! Now I know the two of you. Rory and Mik, right?"

"Yep!" Mik said.

"I felt there was something a little off about the two of you, and I see I am correct."

Mik remembered the man's name was Michael Donnigan, and his home was next to Ramona and Marshall.

Mik said, "You seem to be a good man, Michael. If I remember correctly, you live next to my favorite couple. Regarding all of you, rest assured that I am friends with several community members and would give my life for them or you."

A woman stepped forward, "Rory. I have seen you in my mind but did not understand until this point. I am happy the rock did not ventilate you, as Brigit said."

Rory laughed, "Yeah, I am also quite happy about that!" The others just stared at her. She would explain it to them later.

She said, "I see great and good things in your future," she paused, "These newcomers are our friends. I trust and have faith in them. They have our best interest at hand."

The woman paused momentarily; Rory saw it and knew what it was. Rory whispered to her, "What did you see?"

The woman smiled and spoke, matching the whisper, "Give Brigit and Joseph our love and tell them we miss her dearly."

Rory approached her and whispered, "I will," Rory said.

The woman said, "OH!" She said loudly, "Brigit will be here for lunch tomorrow!"

Mik replied to her, "That is a fact. I truly adore your gift." She looked shocked at his comment. Then, understanding came over her face. Everyone pressed to say hello to the newcomers.

"It seems you understand a great deal about us and our way of life."

"Well. For nearly five years, my education has been considerable. Brigit, Joseph, Gayle, and Jonathon have seen that we understand and support all of you."

Mik and Rory were nearly hugged to death. Evidently, emotion and hugging are currency, and they just got wealthy.

~~~~~~~~~~

Several people were assembled in the square near Brigit's favorite bench.

"This is Rory calling car 324."

"Car 324. Hi, Rory."

"Brigit, a great many people are looking forward to seeing you."

"I have missed them all," The comm was on loud so everyone in the square could hear the entire conversation. No one spoke. They listened intently. Even the birds were somewhat silent at the moment.

"What's your ETA?" Mik asked.

He and Rory spent the night in Ramona and Marshall's home. They had a spare bed that Rory told Mik to use. She slept on the couch. They both slept very well.

"I see my house. I mean, Ramona's house."

Ramona laughed. It was a running joke between them. Through the comm, you could hear Brigit laughing as well.

Rory asked, "Who all is with you?"

"Me, Magda, Joseph, Gayle, and Marcel," she paused a heartbeat. "Jon stayed home to tend to both farms, and Rufus dropped in to help for a few days. Virginia will be arriving in a few hours. Marcel, well, he wanted to keep an eye on you."

Ramona cracked up. Other women close by started laughing as well.

"Uh-huh. Keep an eye on me." Rory said.

Brigit said, "ETA is 90-seconds. Heads up!"

Everyone looked up, and a moment later, Rory pointed. Mik and David came out of the building and joined them, and the rest of the Elders followed.

The car hovered over the square, and people moved around a bit. Brigit maneuvered the vehicle into the area behind the ground car and landed. The engine shut off, and the four doors and the trunk popped open.

Everyone exited. Brigit and Gayle had tears in their eyes and running down their cheeks. It had been a long time since they stood in this place, and they really missed it. Marcel grabbed Rory and gave her a hug and a kiss. Magda got a hug from Ramona.

Mark grabbed Brigit and hugged her, and Brigit hugged Zoee. "Hi, Zoee!" She said.

"Funny, we never met, but I know you."

Brigit said, "You do. We grew up together, and we are close in age. I opted for the fields, and you went for the crafts."

They talked briefly about the old days, and David raised his hand. The square got quiet.

"Friends, this is the first day of our future. These people, our new friends, will help us get there while keeping things as they are meant to be. We will be fine."

Applause and cheering. Next, the biggest party the community has ever seen.

~~~~~~~~~~

The following day, Mik received a call from Virginia.

"Colonel, someone parked a classic in my workspace? A 26 Double L," Virginia asked.

"Wait, a 26 Luxury Lunar? I had no idea any existed. What does it look like?"

"It looks like the images I have pasted to the walls of my office! Same accessories and color scheme, actually."

"Now, V. If that is true, I would look at the registration and see who the owner is. That is a nice car, and it would be bad if they forgot where they parked it." Mik let on that Rory was in the room as well. "Can you believe it, Rory? There's a 26 Double L parked in the station garage?" It was difficult for her not to grin or smile through the call. Thankfully, it was audio only.

Virginia opened the car and sat in the pilot's seat. She tapped the start sequence and opened the registration file. "**WHAT THE HELL!!!**"

"HAPPY BIRTHDAY, V!" Rory and Mik said to her simultaneously.

"Wait, this is mine. I have wanted one of these since I was 4. How…. When…. Where…."

Rory said, "She is such a wonderful speaker."

Mik added, "With such an amazing command of language."

"This is really mine?"

"When you look at the registration file, who is the owner?"

"Me."

"OK, then, you answered your own question. Your orders for the day are to check out your new car, get used to flying it, and go to the Moon and pick up a pizza order. It's paid for already. Bring it here to the community for a 1 PM lunch. I promised a few kids they get to have their first slice of pizza."

"YES, BOSS!"

Mik disconnected and called Tommy.

"Tommy, go make sure Virginia is OK. We gave her a birthday gift, which blew her mind."

"The 26 Double L?"

"Yep, you heard?"

"Hard to keep a secret from me up here on the station. I know everyone."

"Ride with her and join us here at the settlement. She needs a passenger anyway, someone to talk to for sure."

"Will do, Boss."

~~~~~~~~~~

Virginia called Rory and let her know she was landing. Rory went outside, followed by Mik, Brigit, and Marcel.

The car landed perfectly. It is a beautiful car, and the design is somewhat based on the vehicles from the mid-20th century. It is a huge car, twice the length and half again the width of Brigit's car. The paint was precisely what Virginia had on her wall, of this exact car. A vehicle that Victor fixed up, restored, and painted to match the car on the wall above Virginia's desk.

The overall color was a deep, metal flake maroon, and the trim and the roof were gold, appearing to be highly polished as if it was real gold. The interior was brown leather with a comfortable cover over the seats. The electronic package seemed to be a restored set. Still, the software and capability let her know it was a current system, which is safer when flying through space.

After shutting it off, she ran, tackle-hugged Rory and Mik, and kissed them.

Monica saw her landing and made her way there, and by the time the tackled duo stood, Monica said, "I believe she loves her birthday gift."

Virginia grabbed Monica, and they landed in a snow pile laughing.

They brought the pizzas into the barn, where the kids were all waiting.

Time for a pizza-tasting party.

~~~~~~~~~~~

The community has taken to the universe, and Magda has seen they understand what they can and cannot do. The first thing they do is come by the bus load to her station, where they stay for one week and acquire an identity while learning about the universe as it truly is.

Their instructors are Rory and Marcel Romet. Married a few months after the community learned how the universe really is and returned from a whirlwind honeymoon throughout the solar system. They were granted an extended leave by their boss.

Their timeline for the community is simple. The first three years were for the community to experience the universe. In the current year, the fourth year, Magda is considering a few news people to break the story of the community that lives like in the olden times. At least, that is how she plans to portray it to her. She selected a bright, young female and her cameraman to come to the station for an interview. They think it is to announce her retirement.

Retirement. Minikid told her the date she would retire would be easy to know. It is one month after Colonel Mik was promoted to general. She heard from her boss or team of bosses that Mik's promotion was less than a year away. So, when the new year starts, she will retire and turn it all over to Mik.

Virginia and Rory were promoted to Major more than a year ago. Rory left military service a few months later and works as a civilian employee. She actually leads the training team.

Marcel and Mik made O-6 a few years ago. Marcel is a full Captain, and Mik is a Full Colonel. Still, the greatest difference is that Mik wants to make General and have a long career, and Marcel wants to be with Rory and start a family.

Virginia is a Lieutenant Colonel now. Pinning it on four years after making Major. She works directly for Colonel Spencer. Tommy Reilley made Captain and left the job to go home to

Mars. After a few months of tending the gardens, he called Magda and asked if he could work for her, and she jumped at the chance. He is the civilian logistics manager for the outer solar system. This new position needed to be filled with the right person. Mars base is the perfect place for this position.

Brigit and Joseph moved to the newest station in Mars orbit. It is an offshoot of the community and directly under the command of General Spencer and Lieutenant Colonel Rolf. The instructor team, the Romet's, teach here periodically. The station has several levels of fields and livestock. The produce and the animals make their way to the surface of Mars, where they are disbursed to the outer solar system. They have a completely separate group specializing in pets. Joseph has his pet services and veterinary practice on the station. These are dogs, cats, rabbits, and hamsters that can acclimate to the environment of space, a colony, or a station. Several, like over a hundred, pets made their way to the recent colony ship. Joseph told each one what was happening, their name, and their human caretaker. The animals love Joseph, and he feels the same about each of them. Several community members with animal gifts work for Joseph, and Mik is prodding him to be a licensed vet.

Gayle and Jonathan's home is pretty much community property, as in property of the community. Ramona, Mark, Marshall, and Zoee live there full time and help members of the community acclimate to the world, and starting in a few months, a few of the people in the world who want the simpler life and are willing to commit to the life of the community. Ramona and Marshall have the big bedroom, as Jon and Gayle willed it to them. Zoee and Mark travel back and forth, and Zoee has become an excellent pilot in her own right. Mark said if she could drive, he would look out for things not to run into.

Marissa and a few others perform a similar role in the mountains.

Before Joseph and Brigit left for Mars, they gave their home to Rory and Marcel. Teressa had a house waiting for them when they arrived on Mars, and after a year, they moved to the new station. Their cat, Serena, and a dog, the ranch hands named Kiwi, who adopted Joseph while contracting in New Zealand, made the trip to Mars with them. Since they had the car, they used the car to get there in just four hours of flight time. The pets were unhappy they needed to stay in their boxes for the flight, but rules are rules. They have not made a 4-legged space suit yet, but Joseph has that on his list of things to look into once he settles on Mars.

The new skin suits, as Tommy nicknamed them, are fantastic. They have been tested under extreme conditions and are as comfortable as wearing a coat. The helmet will be the next thing to be minimized. The new suit carries a week of life support, as in food, water, and air. It has an efficient evacuation system. The navy fighter pilots will test the suits, and then, if passed, they will go to the general population.

While sleeping one night, Brigit saw that Joseph would attend and graduate from veterinary school on Mars and be a full-service veterinarian. He talked about it for years but does when Mik pushes him. Finishes in record time and loves every minute of the school and the work. He can treat the whole animal. Medical, surgical, emotional, and, of course, psychological.

Gayle and Jonathon enjoy sitting and watching the lives of others unfold. Everyone occasionally gathers at their farm and remembers how things were initially.

Gayle and Jonathon passed on to the next place, but they left the universe a better place on their way.

About the Author

Chris Cancilla was born in the early 1960s in Cleveland, Ohio, on the East Side, in an Italian neighborhood called Collinwood, near East 158th and St. Clair. He really liked growing up there and would not trade it for anything. The friendships he made in Elementary School at

Holy Redeemer and in High School at St. Joseph (now called Villa Angela – St. Joseph's) are priceless, and some are still in force. For most of his youth, he worked in the family business, DiLillo Brothers Dry Cleaners, for his Grandfather Carmen DiLillo and at DiLillo Brothers Men's Wear for his uncle Tony (everyone called him the Czar). He also "apprenticed" with his Uncle Duke, an old-school radio and TV repair shop between the men's wear store and the dry cleaners. But he enjoyed working in the dry cleaners for his Grandfather the most. Two employees, Bertha and Evelyn, were like his second mothers.

In his youth, he really enjoyed Scouting. Spending a significant portion of it in multiple Cub Scout Packs, Boy Scout Troops, and Explorer Posts. Scouting□influenced his life positively, and the training, knowledge, and education he gained during his youth in the troop still influenced his decisions as an adult. The ideals of Scouting, especially the Oath and Law, serve him today as a moral compass, guiding his actions to be a man his family can be proud of in all aspects of his life.

After high school, Chris spent 14 years in the US Air Force, where he saw a large chunk of this 3rd stone from our star. One of his favorite assignments was to Lowry Air Force Base in

Denver, Colorado, where he could ride motorcycles and camp in the Rocky Mountains. This is a close second to the 2 years he was assigned to and lived in Keflavik, Iceland. He and his wife Tammy became best friends and experienced odd and unique landscapes and adventures. One was the SCUBA Diving Club's Founding President at Naval Air Station Keflavik. The name of the club was:

"vörn kafara á Íslandi"

He and his wife Tammy live in Raleigh, North Carolina, close to Wake Forest. He really misses his little buddy and writing partner, his cat, Snip. Snip followed Chris around from room to room. You may or may not see him all the time, but he is always close by. Unfortunately, Snip crossed the rainbow bridge a couple of years ago; he went fast, which was the only consolation. When Chris writes, though, he still is close by. They made a paw print before he was cremated, and that paw print always sits on the desk near the computer.

The Boy Scouts of America is still a part of his life, especially in teaching new adults the skills needed to survive the outdoors and reinforcing how these outdoor skills and habits need to be introduced to the leaders of tomorrow. Leave No Trace camping is a significant part of his instruction and is a philosophy in the conservative style of camping Chris enjoys, if not the only way to ensure an excellent time for you and future campers. Wilderness camping is a great way to decompress and gain insight into what is hidden in the inner recesses of your mind. Sitting around a campfire on a cool or cold night, watching the flames dance, and watching the wood that has given its all to the moment's beauty allows you to reflect on your thoughts and be honest with yourself. The one person you cannot lie to is yourself, so honesty in your head provides nature to clarify all things.

Imagine you are asleep for a moment, and a noise wakes you. You realize you left the Dutch Oven on a picnic table, thinking you would clean it in the morning. Well, you spend the next few hours arguing with a 50-pound raccoon about the cobbler residue in the Dutch Oven on that picnic table, the same Dutch Oven you said you would clean up in the morning. Sometimes, you let the raccoon win!

Chris also has a passion for cooking. Creating several cookbooks allows him to experience new cuisines and cooking methods from around the globe. Still, it also gives him the ability and materials to share and teach cooking to less experienced or knowledgeable people. He does not consider himself a chef, but he does consider himself a somewhat OK cook, both in the home and in the woods.

Cooking in the woods is a skill that not all that many people have even considered. However, it is one skill that Chris enjoys teaching to Scout Leaders, both old and new, in classes he teaches for Scouters (Adult Boy Scout Leaders) and the Scouts themselves during the COOKING Merit Badge. Chris was happy that the BSA finally made cooking a required merit badge for the Eagle Scout rank. It is a skill that will be valuable for the rest of your life. Especially if you want to prepare a romantic meal for a date or simply provide a meal you enjoy.

Whenever Chris develops or finishes a new story or cookbook, he permits some people to read his book and offer ideas to improve the storyline or the text. In addition, he may allow you to be the next editor, for which he will give you kudos at the beginning of the book. Thus immortalizing you in the story for all eternity.

His last hobby is Amateur Radio. In the Raleigh, NC area, you can find him in the mornings on **K4ITL** and in the evenings on **AA4RV**; he pops in occasionally to AK4H. If you use a DMR (Digital Mobile Radio), try to make a QSO with him on the **TGIF Network, Talk Group 1870**. He usually monitors that talk group and would enjoy the QSO.

I hope you enjoyed reading this book. Please read others in the series or check out the cookbooks or both if you are interested in cooking. Also, pick up that briefing booklet if you work with an EDI team and do not understand Electronic Data Interchange. It is well worth your time to read. Reviews of those who previously read the book are in. It is a well-received and informative book that can help someone understand EDI's fantastic and fun world. Tell Chris what you think of the books you read and whether you liked the stories, the briefing, or the recipes.

Chris's day job is as an EDI B2B Integration Specialist or an EDI Developer. Take your pick; they both mean the same thing. He calls himself a digital mailman. He moves the data and information files from one place to another. Still, he does not own, nor is he responsible for, the data in any way other than delivering it.□ So, a mailman! That's a fancy way to tell someone you work with computers to translate data from one format to another. After all, the mailman doesn't write the letters but moves them from point A to B.

Additional Works by
Christopher E. Cancilla

All these titles are available at:
https://AuthorCancilla.com

The Archives,
a 7-Part, Time Travel Novel Series

Revised, edited, and renewed as of October of 2023

EDI Education Series, a 5-Part briefing

providing an understanding of EDI

1. EDI Education: Briefing 1 – Introduction – What is EDI, and how does it work? Read and Learn!
2. EDI Education: Briefing 2 – Deep Dive – A Deeper Dive into the 850/Purchase Order
3. EDI Education: Briefing 3 – Getting Paid – a Deeper understanding of the 810/Invoice
4. EDI Education: Briefing 4 – Shipping – Demystifying the 856/Advance Ship Notice
5. EDI Education: Briefing 5 – The Complete Briefing – A review of the first 4 books with additional insight

Free to Read Stories

available on http://AuthorCancilla.com

1. Stargate Universe
2. Scorpion Sting
3. Terra Nova

Additional Science Fiction books available

1. The Ultimate Thru-Hike
2. Bus Route 40-A
3. Lost Earth
4. Colony 3

Books in the Brigit Markz series

1. **Mountain Life** – *Book one in the Brigit Markz series*
2. **Life in Transition** – *Book two in the Brigit Markz series*
3. **Home Life** – Book three in the Brigit Markz series

Other available books and novels

1. AMMO – IYAAYAS
2. Toasting Marshmallows on my Dumpster Fire
3. Getting Published
4. Getting Published Two
5. Life as an Amateur
6. Stories from Time and Space
7. Scouting and Camping: A New Parents Guide
8. Scouting to Summer Camp
9. Camp Menu Planning
10. Personal Menu Planning
11. Learning to Camp
12. Packing your Backpack for a 5-Day Trip

Discounts and Deals

For current and available discounts, go to
http://AuthorCancilla.com

1. ARCHIVE: the 7-part series
2. EDI: The Complete Briefing
3. Learning to Camp and Learning to Backpack
4. June of 2024 – Complete three book Brigit Markz series

Made in the USA
Columbia, SC
28 March 2024

33654670R00141